Fly Away, Cinda

Books By Janet Lambert
by year of original publication

PENNY PARRISH STORIES
Star Spangled Summer 1941
Dreams of Glory 1942
Glory Be! 1943
Up Goes the Curtain 1946
Practically Perfect 1947
The Reluctant Heart 1950

TIPPY PARRISH STORIES
Miss Tippy 1948
Little Miss Atlas 1949
Miss America 1951
Don't Cry Little Girl 1952
Rainbow After Rain 1953
Welcome Home, Mrs. Jordon 1953
Song in Their Hearts 1956
Here's Marny 1969

JORDON STORIES
Just Jennifer 1945
Friday's Child 1947
Confusion by Cupid 1950
A Dream for Susan 1954
Love Taps Gently 1955
Myself & I 1957
The Stars Hang High 1960
Wedding Bells 1961
A Bright Tomorrow 1965

PARRI MACDONALD STORIES
Introducing Parri 1962
That's My Girl 1964
Stagestruck Parri 1966
My Davy 1968

CANDY KANE STORIES
Candy Kane 1943
Whoa, Matilda 1944
One for the Money 1946

DRIA MEREDITH STORIES
Star Dream 1951
Summer for Seven 1952
High Hurdles 1955

CAMPBELL STORIES
The Precious Days 1957
For Each Other 1959
Forever and Ever 1961
Five's a Crowd 1963
First of All 1966
The Odd Ones 1969

SUGAR BRADLEY STORIES
Sweet as Sugar 1967
Hi, Neighbor 1968

CHRISTIE DRAYTON STORIES
Where the Heart Is 1948
Treasure Trouble 1949

PATTY AND GINGER STORIES
We're Going Steady 1958
Boy Wanted 1959
Spring Fever 1960
Summer Madness 1962
Extra Special 1963
On Her Own 1964

CINDA HOLLISTER STORIES
Cinda 1954
Fly Away Cinda 1956
Big Deal 1958
Triple Trouble 1965
Love to Spare 1967

FLY AWAY, CINDA

by Janet Lambert

Image Cascade Publishing
www.ImageCascade.com

MANUFACTURED IN THE UNITED STATES
OF AMERICA

A hardcover edition of this book was originally published by E. P. Dutton & Co. It is here reprinted by arrangement with Mrs. Jeanne Ann Vanderhoef.

First *Image Cascade Publishing* edition published 2003.

Library of Congress Cataloging in Publication Data
Lambert, Janet, 1895–1973.
Fly away Cinda.

(Juvenile Girls)
Reprint. Originally published: New York: E. P. Dutton, 1956.

ISBN 1-930009-92-5 (Pbk.)

For

GWYNNE

Brant Beach, New Jersey
July 16, 1956

Dear, dear girls:

It has been a long time since I have had a chat with you. But you must know how constantly you are in my thoughts, because I've sent you several more books, always guided by your written wishes.

Some of you write, "Please tell us more about Tippy," some want to hear of Dria, Cinda, Penny, Susan, or Carrol, and many of you have wondered, "Whatever became of Candy Kane?" So my thoughts hop from one character to another while I consider your letters, then settle on whichever story the majority of you has asked for.

A Song in Their Hearts (the last book I sent off to you) had another title when I began writing it. I had planned to find out what I could for all of us about Tippy and Peter Jordan, down in Panama, and was as surprised as I'm sure you were to have dear Candy and funny, difficult Barton turn up there, too. So, naturally, they came into the story, and a new title had to be found to include them. I'm quite sure it all happened because your letters about Candy kept popping into my thoughts!

I do hope you won't mind that the next book will be about a new family. I'm writing it now, not because I've lost interest in the characters I love so much, but because...truly, girls, do you think Penny, Tippy, and Candy are growing a little too old for you to enjoy? Even Dria Meredith is eighteen, and Susan Jordan is almost that.

I've worried over it. So, while I haven't had a single letter asking to meet a new family, I postponed the story I had intended to write about Susan, and, all of my own initiative, discovered the Campbells, instead.

It's quite a problem. I know your letter will solve it for me, just as they always have, and we can take another peek at Susan while she struggles with that rather discouraging Bobby Parrish (who refuses to be discouraged), or can meet interesting new people. There are so many interesting people in the world, whole families of them, that it really doesn't matter to me which you decide.

And thank you again for your letters. You're almost like Santa Claus's helpers, aren't you? For even though you never receive credit for writing the books, I know what a large part you play in the making of them, and am always,

devotedly and gratefully,

Dear Readers:

Mother always said she wanted her books to be good enough to be found in someone's attic!

After all of these years, I find her stories—not in attics at all—but prominent in fans' bookcases just as mine are. It is so heart-warming to know that through these republications she will go on telling good stories and being there for her "girls," some of whom find no other place to turn.

With a heart full of love and pride–
Janet Lambert's daughter,
Jeanne Ann Vanderhoef

Fly Away, Cinda

Chapter I

MRS. HOLLISTER looked through the long front window at the glistening, snow-covered lawn, then back at her desk clock; and put down her pen. Three-thirty. It was time for the front door to begin its after-school banging, so she pushed aside the Christmas cards she had been writing and sat, expectantly waiting.

Buff would skip along the front porch first, her short skirt looking like a plaid umbrella over her snow pants, her light curls swirled neatly out from under a knitted hood, the ends of her plaid scarf folded back, just so, over the shoulders of her navy blue coat. She would say, "Hello, Mother, I'm home," in a polite little voice, present her spelling paper with its customary "100" marked at the top in red pencil, then proceed daintily on to the kitchen and the big cookie jar that Stella, the cook, tried to keep filled.

Bobo would tramp in next. The pattern rarely varied, for the two youngest Hollisters had good appetites and small allowances. Bobo, who had been christened the very nice name of Blair—which no one ever used—never had any money. Buff, who had started out a quickly-forgotten Elizabeth, was too penurious to part with any of hers. So they always hustled home and reported their afternoon plans in person, instead of telephoning from the drugstore.

Bobo was sure to yell, "Hi, Mom," in a shrill scream that pierced the eardrums. His heavy jacket might be hanging open or buttoned crooked, his cords might be filthy at the knees, and he might have one glove on or have lost them both, but his hair was sure to be so neatly combed that little paths ran through it. At thirteen, snub-nosed Bobo had suddenly become so enamored of greasy hair lotions that he would rather have all the buttons off his shirt than no comb in its pocket.

It would be at least four-thirty before Cinda came; Cinda, who was a lovely sixteen, and always brought two or three chattering girls home with her. After a cup of hot chocolate in a small café across from the high school, the girls would dash in, pile their coats in the hall, and, still talking endlessly and all together, run up the stairs for secret conferences in Cinda's room. Mrs. Hollister loved to hear the bursts of laughter that floated down.

Lindsey would come last. After basketball practice, he would swoop his old car into the driveway and park it so exactly by the side steps that his father, tired from a day in his law office or in court, would have to draw up behind it and walk across the lawn in the snow.

It always happened that way. At a quarter to six the front door always opened and a resigned voice groaned, "By all the gods, Fran, he's done it again. Can't that boy walk an extra foot?" And in summer it was worse. Warren was home from Princeton then, and two old cars, plus the family station wagon, usurped so much of the driveway that Donald J. Hollister's sedan barely cleared the front sidewalk.

Without really seeing it, Frances Hollister looked out at the soft white blanket that covered the whole state of New Jersey, thinking about her children. She, who disliked nicknames, had five young people answering to them.

Steady, brilliant Warren, who knew he wanted to be a lawyer as quickly as possible, was called War-Horse. Lindsey was Jinx; happy-go-lucky Jinx, who wanted only to play football, baseball, and basketball, and still make decent enough grades to graduate in June. And there was Melinda Cynthia.

Mrs. Hollister smiled a little as she thought of the terrible combination of names she had given her third-born. Naming one baby for two grandmothers had been a mistake, especially since, somehow, the name had been registered backwards, with the Cynthia grandmother tacked on the end and hurt to the quick. Shortening the unfortunate combination to Cynda had been a happy solution that had restored peace; and spelling it with a *y* had helped, too, for a time. But when a minister had mispronounced the name and christened the poor baby something that rhymed with "signed-a," even Grandmother Hollister had admitted it was quite unreadable and had suggested a more acceptable spelling. War-Horse, Jinx, Cinda, Bobo, and Buff.

Footsteps sounded on the porch, and she turned her head expectantly, ready to receive either of the little ones. But it was Cinda who opened the door.

"Hi, sweetie," Cinda called. "What are you doing, home alone on a Tuesday? What happened to your bridge foursome?"

"Colds and sick children." Her mother laughed ruefully, and asked, "Wouldn't you know it? Just when I had all of mine perpendicular for the first time in three weeks?"

"It was a mean trick of fate to keep you in on such a gorgeous day."

Cinda pulled off the bright wool scarf that covered her hair and smoothed her brown curls. Her eyes, big, just as brown and dark-fringed as her mother's, sparkled softly as she grinned and said, "Oh, well, it's nice to have you around. I'm sort of in your fix. Barbie had to go to the dentist, Kitty Lou's mother picked her up, and Mart had to stay after school on newspaper business." She laid a stack of books on a table, stuffed her scarf into her coat pocket and dropped the coat on a chair, then exclaimed good-naturedly. "Oops, sorry," and picked it up. "Yes'm," she said before her mother could speak, "I know where the coat closet is. But I have news to pass on. Miss Alexander," she announced, "is going to be married. We're to have a new English teacher after the holidays, because she's going to marry a man with three kids."

"No!"

"Yep. One of 'em's in Buff's class. She's a scrawny little kid and certainly needs a mother. Which reminds me," she said, coming into the living room and still holding the coat, "I met Buff on my way home. After great agony of mind, she's decided to part with a dime. She and that screechy little Charmion Ayer are going to blow themselves to small portions of fudge sundaes at Peterson's. And she said to tell you that you fluffed Bobo's arithmetic problems again, so he'll have to stay after school and do them over."

"I *told* him not to trust me!" her mother wailed. "I never could do arithmetic, and I begged him to wait for your father, but he talked me into believing that the answers in the back of the book didn't fit the problems we did. Who," she asked, changing to a happier subject, "is Miss Alexander going to marry?"

"Mr. Carter, or Crater, or something. He has an automobile agency."

"For goodness' sake! I know him. It's Mr. Calder."

Cinda was about to return to the hall when her mother hopped up and asked eagerly, "Are you going to stay home now?"

"I guess so. Why?"

"I thought I might run next door and tell Ellie Mason the good news. Mr. Calder is such a nice man and people have felt so sorry for him since his wife died, and have been trying to marry him off to dozens of girls. But I don't want the children to come home to an empty house."

She paused for breath, and Cinda asked, "Where's Stella?"

"Over at her sister's. I thought I was going to be here."

Mrs. Hollister was eager for release, so Cinda draped the coat over her shoulders when she reached the archway. " 'Now bundle up good and warm,' " she mimicked, pulling out the scarf and swathing her mother's head in it. " 'And stay on the walk so your feet won't get wet.' "

They looked much alike, standing together. The same brown hair and creamy skin, each with a few left-over summer freckles dotting a short straight nose, each with full, generous lips. But Cinda was taller. The alpaca coat hung almost to her mother's ankles.

"Go on, runt," she teased lovingly.

"Skinny," her mother retorted, pushing up the scarf so she could see.

"I'll dig out the Christmas ornaments and sort them while you're gone. They're always in a mess."

"I know it. I always vow I'll put them away more neatly, but when the day after New Year's comes along I'm so tired of pine needles dripping all over the carpet that Stella and I just pitch them into boxes." Mrs. Hollister gave a deprecating shrug at her inefficiency and asked, "You know where they are, don't you?"

"Yep. Up on third, under the shelves in the big storage closet. Scoot."

Cinda held the door open, closed it after her mother and went back to stand in the living room. Once it had been known as the "parlor," and the equally large room behind it had been elegantly referred to as "the music room." The grand piano was still there but the walls had been lined with bookshelves, and the ceiling, once decorated with hand-painted cupids waving garlands of roses at each other, was now a plain light gray to match the carpeting. Comfortable furniture had replaced the spindly French chairs and cabinets, and a wide archway instead of "folding doors" made the two rooms seem almost one. The Christmas tree would stand, as it had for four generations, before the plate glass windows overlooking the kitchen wing and a portion of the back yard.

The house had been built in the early nineteen hundreds by Cinda's great-grandfather, and the Hollisters casually called it "the horror." Dark red stone formed its solid lower half, bulging out to encompass a wide semicircular porch. Dark red shingles went up, up to a slate roof with a fancy cupola on one end, and small-paned windows peeked out below the wide eaves. The house was three stories high, definitely Victorian, ugly, and of no particular style, but so comfortable and roomy that they wouldn't have traded it for any other house in Glenvale. In fact, they couldn't believe their good fortune when the senior Hollisters had decided to move to an apartment hotel, and had transferred the deed to their only son.

The hall, or the "reception hall," as Grandmother Hollister still called it, had long since lost its formality. It was still large and square and had a brick fireplace; but a fireside bench made an excellent seat for corn popping or for warming cold toes, and a gold-framed mirror above the mantel and the ornate hatrack were gone. The staircase, however, wide and made of beautiful oak, was the same.

Cinda loved the stairway with its two landings and high, stained glass windows. Their leaded pattern was inset with jewels; and while the jewels were made only of colored glass, they caught the light like rubies, emeralds, sapphires, and diamonds.

I guess we'll have to keep the tree in the same old place, she reflected, starting up the steps. Gramps would have a fit if we moved it up front where people could see it from the street. The wreaths with red bows have to hang there.

Bright colors bathed her all the way to the second floor, and even when she opened the door which led to the enormous third floor room, where Hollisters had always given their gayest parties. The great-grandparents had entertained their euchre club there, Gramps and Gram their progressive bridge, Frances and Donald Hollister often had friends up to dance, and the younger group played table tennis, had soft drinks from a small refrigerator in a closet, and kept a record player going. Cinda thought this room was the second-nicest in the whole house; Warren's was the nicest.

By right of juvenile seniority, Warren had the tower room. He had privacy and his own bath. And he had windows that looked out over the world. With a table and two padded maple chairs in his cupola, he was a king. Cinda opened the door to the room which had stood empty for a year and a half, and wished Warren would bestow the right of temporary occupancy upon her. She would gladly move out for a week end now and then, or even for long vacations, and would offer more storage space in the closets than Warren reluctantly surrendered. He was fussy about having boxes and out-of-season garments put in his closets under the eaves, and he kept one padlocked.

Cinda went to the one where the Christmas tree ornaments lived for eleven months and two weeks out of each year, and, looking in, decided Warren had justification for his stinginess. Her mother was a hoarder. The cardboard cartons were hidden behind a pile of old hats, shoes, tennis rackets, and a hodgepodge of mismatched china.

It took a long time to drag them out, still longer to carry them downstairs, two big cartons at a time; and on her last trip she began to wish Hollisters had gone in for shorter, skinnier trees. So many strings of lights, so many boxes of bright, delicate balls, such wads of tinsel.

But seated on the floor in the library, sorting began to be fun. Out came the angel of Warren's babyhood, a bird with a spun-glass tail that marked Lindsey's first Christmas, and she was smoothing out the tinsel framing her own special star when the hall door let in a draft of cold air, and Lindsey came in.

"Gosh, we aren't going to trim the tree *this* early, are we?" he demanded, tossing his heavy jacket on the fireside bench and coming to stand above her.

"I'm sorting things out to see how much we'll have to buy," she answered. "Remember this?"

She held up a red cotton Santa Claus, and he grinned. "Kind of beat-up, isn't he?" he said, taking the little figure and trying to straighten the thin, misshapen legs. "Poor guy, he's as old as Dad."

Lindsey was the stocky one of the family. His wide shoulders could block a tackle so hard that the impact jarred his opponent, even through protective padding; his muscular right arm could send a baseball flying in from center field, and he was formidable on a basketball court. In school, however, he was proud to be in "the bright half of the dumb section," and would grin amiably when his father scowled at a report card which was poor, but never quite poor enough to mean failure. His wide hazel eyes usually mirrored merriment, and his brown hair would have been the color of Cinda's had he ever let it grow long enough to show any color. Lindsey was a happy soul; and few people outside his own family knew how sensitive he was, or how loving.

"Catch," he said, tossing the Santa Claus and flopping into his father's favorite red leather chair.

"How come you're home so early?"

She gave him several strings of lights to untangle, and he answered with a shrug, "Coach had the sneezes. We kidded around a while, then left. I might ask you the same."

"Nothing else to do. Moth went next door to the Mason's. Jinx," Cinda crossed her legs, rested one elbow on her knee and cupped her chin in the palm of her hand as she asked, "do you suppose War-Horse would let me use the tower room while he's away?"

"Over my dead body." He scowled at the lights, tossed her a free string, and added, "I've been considering moving up there."

"But you'll be away next year, too," she protested. "I could enjoy it for a whole year and a half. I could sit up there and –dream."

"*Dream*?" Lindsey stared at her. Cinda never had been the dreamy type. Busy, babbling, excitable, yes. But a dreamer? "Oh, no!" he said.

"I do it lots of times. I sit and think, and think, and think," she contended.

"What about–clothes?"

"Sometimes. But usually . . . " She became honestly serious as she explained, "Lots of times I think about myself. I wonder if I'm a misfit–if there's anything *to* me, really. I keep getting on people's nerves and the family always thinks my opinions are sort of flighty; so I wonder if people don't appreciate me or if I'm all wrong. Don't you ever wonder that?"

"Maybe–no, I guess not." Lindsey coiled another string of

lights, twisted its cord around to make it a figure eight, and tucked an end through to hold it. "When you're keen on athletics," he said, dropping it down beside him, "you know you're never so good that you couldn't be better. You accept it."

"But outside of athletics—don't you ever wonder if girls like you? Aren't you ever worried for fear they might think you're sort of . . . well—awkward? Or not quick enough on the upswing?"

"Not too much." She was leaning closer to him, and Lindsey, who secretly doubted that he had any charm whatever, so had developed a goodhumored ridicule of himself and a bluff heartiness, became busy with his lights again. Only Warren knew why Lindsey lived down to the name of Jinx—and a girl named Paula understood, a little. "I don't have time to worry about girls," he said.

"But suppose you did," Cinda persisted artlessly, anxious to know the male reaction to her type, "suppose you were simply mad about dancing. Would you ask me to go to a dance?"

"Gosh, no! You're my sister."

"But suppose I weren't. Or suppose you were someone else. Just suppose you were—well, Al Kennedy. If you were Al, would you ask me?"

"Are you revved up over him?" Lindsey looked up and studied her, but she shook her head.

"I only picked him," she said, grinning, "because he's the quarterback on your football team. I used to think he was dreamy, but . . . " She stopped and made a little face. "Last spring," she said disgustedly, "he went with our gang to a carnival. We ate popcorn and candy and ice cream cones, and —and he whoopsed in our front yard. I haven't been able to *look* at him since."

"Just because he whoopsed?" Lindsey was incredulous. "I never heard of anything so dumb. If I got a beef on every guy who chucked his cookies before a game . . . "

"But this wasn't a game, and I keep seeing inside his stomach," Cinda interrupted. "He isn't a hero to me any more. He has a weak stomach."

"Well, my gosh, that's a dilly! It gives me a pat answer to your question, too. If I were Al Kennedy, I definitely would not ask you to go to a dance."

His tone held such withering scorn that she said in a small contrite voice, "I'm sorry. But if you were someone else–Page Vandergren, for instance–would you–then?"

"I gather he hasn't."

"Well . . . not yet."

"And that's the real pitch." He finished his last string of lights, dropped it on the pile, and leaned back. "My child," he said in a fatherly tone, "I will give you advice."

"You needn't," she declared hotly, jerking tinsel from a box and watching a red ornament bounce out and break. "I only used Page as another example. He has a good stomach–but he has pimples on his chin."

She knew he hadn't. He had a firm, unblemished chin; but Lindsey seemed as unaware of Page's handsome exterior as he had been of Al's unreliable stomach, for he was saying, "Suppose we take it from the guy's point of view. Could be that *you* aren't exactly appealing."

"That's what I was afraid of," she sighed.

"You're pretty. Don't bother to say 'thank you,' " he forestalled her pleased smile, "because you have bad habits. You sit and twist your hair."

"Huh?"

"A lock of it. When you talk to anybody, you sit and

twist, and twist, and twist. It makes you look kind of simple."

"Well, goodness me!"

"Lots of girls do it, and it's as bad as a fellow picking at his shoelaces because he doesn't know what else to do with his hands. Pick, pick, twist, twist. Bobo picks and you twist. It drives me nuts."

"I'll stop right away." She nodded, and asked earnestly, "Is there anything else I do wrong?"

"Yeah, you gabble a lot and put on lipstick downstairs," he went on, ruthlessly trampling her small amount of ego. "And the way you shriek '*utterly!*' Everything is 'simply utterly . . .' Half the time you don't bother to put any more words on the end. But," he added, pitying her embarrassment, "on the whole, you're not so bad."

"Well, I should certainly think she isn't!"

Both heads turned to find Buff standing in the living room, her hands on the hips of her plaid jumper dress. "The very idea," she lectured in a voice so like her mother's that they grinned, "of criticizing your sister!"

"He was only telling me how to be more glamorous, Buff," Cinda laughed, finding an end on her wad of tinsel and pulling it out. "How to wow the boys."

"Gracious, does he have to?" Buff walked daintily in and said with complete assurance, "I should think you'd know when you're attractive."

"I don't, always. Do you?" Cinda laid the tinsel in her lap and waited expectantly while Buff smiled her white, even little smile.

"Of course," Buff said, her head back and her blue eyes wide. "I always know I'm the most attractive child in the room."

"Oh, you don't!"

"Yes, I do. I never giggle the way Charmion does when I say 'how-do-you-do' to people, and I always have the most partners at dancing school, and everyone always says, 'What a lovely child.' "

"Can you beat it?" Cinda shook her head at Lindsey and said, amazed, "She'll never need to sit in the tower room and think. She's analyzed herself early."

"Oh, I wouldn't want to. It's too lonesome and cold up there." Buff dropped on the carpet and arranged her pleats neatly about her. "Please." she asked, "may I help?"

"With my blessing." Cinda tossed another tangle of tinsel into Buff's lap and wondered why God had chosen to send such a strange little creature to the Hollisters. Buff was so different from the rest of them. She was a combination of adult vanity and childish whimsies; a fairylike little thing who knew she was a lovely fairy and enjoyed watching herself in a mental mirror. With her fair head bent and her fingers flying deftly, she unsnarled more knots and put more ornaments in their rightful boxes than the others did.

"There," she said, reaching for the last lid, just as Bobo floundered in and stepped on it. "My, but you're an awkward boy. It's a good thing we finished our work before you and Down Boy came home and ruined everything. Have you fed him?"

"Sure."

Down Boy was a boxer that had tried the Hollisters' patience for over two years. He had been so happy to be chosen from a litter of five handsome puppies, and so exuberant over his good fortune that, for the first week, no one had addressed him without shouting, "Down, boy, down boy! *Down*!" Eventually, since no name could be found to suit him and since he responded to no commands, Down Boy became his formal mode of address.

It worked two ways. It called him to them, yet kept his four feet on the ground.

"Stella's feeding him," Bobo volunteered, peeking into all the boxes and leaving the lids on crooked. "Where's Mom?"

"At the Mason's." Cinda heard the front door open and slid around to see into the hall.

Her mother and father had come in together. Their arms were linked and they were laughing; but she was sure she saw her mother look up at their big, handsome father and wink, as if to give him his cue, for he yelled dutifully,

"By all the gods, Fran, that boy has done it again!"

Chapter II

LINDSEY waited comfortably in the red leather chair while his father hung up his overcoat and hat, even while he passed through the living room and paused to glance at the headlines on the evening paper. Then, at the last second before his father reached him, he shoved to his feet and invited cordially, "Have a seat and rest your frazzled nerves. I meant to put the car away tonight—my intentions were strictly noble—but I plead extenuating circumstances. Mom's car was parked ahead of me."

"With no keys in it, I suppose?"

"Well, yes, could be." Lindsey knew his mother always forgot to remove her keys from the ignition lock, so he said, "But it would have meant getting out of my car, walking to Mom's, getting in, driving it into her half of the garage, getting out, walking back to mine, getting in, driving it to its parking spot beside the hedge, getting out, walking back . . . "

"You exhaust me." His father sat down, accepted the light touch of Buff's lips against his cheek, smoothed down his sandy-blond hair before she could, and watched Lindsey watch Cinda carry the cardboard cartons out to the service pantry. "If you feel sufficiently rested after your arduous day," he suggested mildly, "it might be a good idea for you to put all three cars away. We aren't going out tonight, are we, Fran?" he asked his wife.

"Not that I know of."

Mrs. Hollister moved Bobo away from the bookshelves to reach for her knitting bag, and he gave an extra bounce of his own as he asked eagerly, "Could I help, Dad? Could I drive one of the cars to the garage?"

"You may not."

Both adult Hollisters answered together, and Buff added, "Mercy, but you can ask stupid questions. You don't know how to *drive* a car!"

"I got to learn, don't I?" he contested. "When I get old enough to inherit a car I gotta be ready."

"Pooh." Buff sidestepped for Lindsey who was on his way out, and said sweetly, "There probably won't be any more left to inherit. Mother gave hers to War-Horse instead of turning it in, and Gramps passed his on to Jinx. I don't see where you'll ever get one, because Dadda's is the expensive kind that never wears out." And she offered winsomely, "I'll hold your yarn for you, Mother, dear, if you want to wind it."

"No, thank you, darling." Mrs. Hollister patted Bobo's smooth head before she sat down and consoled, "Don't worry, pet. Four or five years from now there may be an ancient model around somewhere. You'll get it."

"Truly, Mom?"

His face lighted up, and such a beautiful dream of anticipation shone in his eyes that she said, "Truly." And she hated to add, "If your finances are good enough to carry heavy insurance and pay for license plates and repairs. Warren and Lindsey worked three summers at the shore to save enough."

"I'll start right away," he promised. "Maybe I could get a job after school as a delivery boy, on my bicycle, huh? I'll bet Mr. Peterson needs a boy to take medicine to sick people."

His father sent a worried frown across his newspaper, but his mother shook her head, smiling. "You know, Bobo," she pointed out, lifting red wool from her knitting bag and inspecting a half-made sweater, "you already owe me two-and-a-half weeks' back allowance. Lindsey shoveled all the snow because you had a Scout meeting, and Down Boy would starve to death if Stella didn't feed him. Trash would be stacked a mile high, too."

"Oh." He looked unhappy. His whole dream had collapsed like a parachute and dropped him right into the middle of a lecture. Before his father, too; and, even worse, before the virtuous Buff.

Buff never failed to keep her room in order, or to carry out the dishes for Stella. She received her fifty cents every Saturday morning, walked straight upstairs, moved one of the staring dolls from the line on her window seat, and dropped the money into her well-hidden and well-filled bank. Buff would be able to afford a car long before he would.

"I don't want any old beat-up sedan," he muttered, thrusting his hands into his pockets and trying to look contemptuous. "War-Horse and Jinx look silly riding around in old sedans with four doors and seat covers. I guess I'll save up for something sportier—maybe a Jaguar."

"And I'll help you, Bobo." Buff secretly adored Blair, and repeatedly told her wary friends that he was "a very wonderful boy." She even loaned him a nickel now and then, under duress and after a hand to hand battle; and sometimes, as now, she unexpectedly sprang to his defense. "I'll help you save," she planned, careful not to involve herself in extra work. "And by the time you're in college we'll have a *real* car."

"Naw." College was too far away; he hadn't finished the eighth grade, yet. So he slouched past Buff and tossed off indifferently, "Well, I guess I'd better wash before dinner."

"Great heavens," Mrs. Hollister said, looking after him and

clicking her needles, "he must have been dying to get out of here, to risk contact with soap and water." She listened to a timid tap on the library door next to the dining room, and called, "All right, Stella, we're coming," then laid down her bright wool.

Dinner started at the Hollisters just as it always did. Chairs scraped on the Oriental rug; Mr. Hollister stood with bent head above the platter and tureens before him, while Lindsey, whose turn it was to say grace, hustled through it. Then everyone sat down and Stella pushed open the pantry door to make her usual apologies for the meal.

"The mashed potatoes'll have lumps in them tonight," she predicted dolefully, smoothing back her neat gray hair and looking about to cry. "I didn't put enough milk in them."

"They're beautiful, Stella." The potatoes rose in fluffy white mounds on each plate Mr. Hollister served, and he sent her a smile of comfort. For almost twenty years he had had to prop up Stella's wilting courage before he could taste his food, so that by now the words came automatically, followed by a pleasant chorus from the other diners. There had been times, when the children were small, that they had failed in their part of the ritual and chattered through it, but tears in the kitchen afterward had trained them far better than parental reminders. So they all chirped dutifully and the meal began.

It followed its usual pattern so completely that in the middle of dessert the telephone rang, and both parents laid down their spoons.

"Really," Mrs. Hollister sighed, watching Lindsey hop up faster than Cinda could, "I do wish your friends would synchronize their meals with ours."

The library door was open; and she listened to Lindsey say,

"Sure, I'll take it," pause, then add a genial, "Hi. No kiddin'! O.K., I'll pass it on."

He laid the receiver on the wide window sill and came back to announce, "That's War-Horse, calling collect. He needs more wampum—money, to you. To buy gas and get home from college. He wants to talk to you, Mom."

"Well, dear me." A collect call from Warren was no novelty, but a request for money was. Mrs. Hollister fluttered in to the telephone, and nothing but surprised exclamations fluttered back.

The family, listening in the dining room, could make no sense of them, so Blair finished his dessert, went out to the kitchen for a second serving, and Buff began a pleasant daydream about letting her hair grow so long she could sit on it. The other three waited patiently for Mrs. Hollister to come back.

"He has me all confused," she finally murmured, standing beside the table and running her hand through her hair in a puzzled way. "He doesn't need money—though perhaps he does, if his bank balance is what he thinks it is. But I don't see how I can have an extra boy here through the holidays."

"What boy?" Lindsey asked.

"Someone he knows who lives in the Philippines, or Bangkok, or some strange place, and can't go home. It's such an inconvenient time for Warren to feel sorry for somebody—just when I'd had a letter from Cousin Maud. I'd planned to put Warren in with Lindsey and give Maud the tower room—so she could go on writing her book, you know, in peace and quiet. Now . . ."

"Frannie." Her husband turned his chair away from the table and pulled her to him. "Give us the story straight," he begged. "We gather that Warren wants to bring a friend home with him, but what does Maud Landis have to do with it?"

"Lots." She sat down on his lap, sidewise, so she could face the others, and said with two worried little creases between her brows, "I had a note from Maud today, saying she has to come to New York to see her publisher, and would love to spend a few days with us. Of course I whipped one right back and said to plan to be with us over Christmas—she and Paula."

"Paula?" Lindsey's heart beat like a roll of drums. Paula would be here for Christmas! Then it skipped a beat and felt as if it would never start again. War-Horse would be here, too.

"I don't know definitely about Paula," his mother was saying. "Maud said she might prefer to spend the holidays with her parents, rather than go traipsing around with an aunt. But she does want to see some shows and she enjoys being with you children, so . . . I thought," she broke off to say, "that it would be nice for poor Maud to have her again. Ever since Paula's mother remarried and Paula has been so happy to have a father, poor Maud has been left out. I really didn't want to discuss it until I was sure they were coming, and when I suddenly realized how far Colorado is from here and how long a letter takes, even an air mail, I called Maud up. I think they're coming. I think so," she repeated. "If they can get plane reservations. And now there's this—this Filipino."

"Are you sure he's one?" Cinda asked, trying to remember just how Filipinos looked, in pictures of them she had seen. Curly-haired, she thought, and short, and very, very thin. Or maybe she had them confused with East Indians and Mahatma Gandhi.

"No, he may be Siamese," her mother sighed, "or Chinese. Anyway, he's something foreign. And what will I do with poor Maud?"

"I suppose it didn't occur to you," her husband suggested mildly, putting his arm around her, "to tell Warren he should hold back his invitation for a day or two, until you found out how much room you had?"

"Naturally not," she replied indignantly. "His poor little friend has no place to go. What would he do in a strange country, on Christmas?" she demanded.

"*I'd* go to Florida," Lindsey answered promptly. "I'd stay in a swell hotel, and swim and lie in the sun. I'd never spend it in New Jersey, from choice."

A discussion of the prospective guest's finances started. Lindsey was certain he must be rich if he could travel all the way to Princeton for an education; Cinda reminded him that Warren always brought home stray dogs, cats, or people; and everyone was voicing an opinion when a high, frightening scream came from the kitchen.

Napkins were flung on the table, a chair tipped over as the Hollisters crowded through a swinging door and the service pantry in a united front.

Stella was standing by the stove, holding one hand out from her flat chest and moaning. Down Boy peeped out from under a table and apologetically wagged what little tail he had.

"What is it, Stella? What happened?" Mrs. Hollister cried, as they all pushed close to her.

"I was pouring the grease out of the skillet," Stella groaned. "I'd heated it again so I could pour it into the coffee tin I keep for my birds, and . . . " She looked down into the mournful eyes pleading with her from under the table. "I jiggled the pan," she moaned loyally, "and hot grease spilled over my hand. I don't know how I ever happened to be so clumsy."

Down Boy knew. The melting grease had smelled so good that his front paws had lost contact with the linoleum. He watched ready tears roll down Stella's cheeks and whimpered a little with her, both in sympathy for her and for the spot on his own nose that was burned. She was the only one who heard him; and since he was her darling, the good companion of her lonely heart, she whispered, "Don't cry, Boy," while she submitted to having an antiseptic salve spread over the reddening surface.

"There's no more in the tube," Mr. Hollister said, squeezing, pressing. "This is enough for now, but we should put a fresh dressing on in an hour or so. How does it feel, Stella?"

"The pain's stopping." Stella watched Mrs. Hollister take a gauze pad from the first aid kit she kept on the pantry shelf, and gave a gasping little sob as it was laid gently over the burns. "I'm such a lot of trouble," she sighed, the tears spurting again. "I wouldn't blame you if you fired me for this."

She was always sure she was about to be "fired." Even after twenty years of praise and the greatest consideration, she was still afraid that, at any minute, she might be pitched out into the world again, with no Hollisters to love her. She sincerely believed she deserved such a fate; and there were moments when, in exasperation, Mrs. Hollister believed it, too.

"I'll run down and get another tube," Cinda said, while her mother offered Stella staunch assurance that misfortune came to everyone and that Buff and Bobo would consider it a pleasure to do the dishes alone, that she was their dearly loved Stella and must let the ironing go, tomorrow.

The whole family knew that mentioning the ironing had been a mistake. Neither sleet, snow, nor an incapacitated hand could delay the ironing. Stella would protest it until the last Hollister had thought up some excuse to leave.

"Want company?" Jinx asked, seizing the opportunity to

bow out quickly, and following Cinda into the hall. "I can drive you."

But she shook her head. "I'd rather walk," she answered. "It's lovely in the starlight, with the snow cold and white and crusty." She took her snow boots from the closet, and inquired as she sat down to put them on, "Are you glad Paula might come for Christmas?"

"I don't know. It's all right, I suppose. Are you?"

"Not particularly." She stamped her foot, ran up a zipper and said, "It's fun having her down on the island in the summer, living practically next door to us, but I'd planned to do a lot of things this vacation that she doesn't like to do. You know, skiing, skating, going out to the old mill for a coasting party and cooking our supper. Paula's not the type who likes to be exposed to the elements."

"War-Horse and I'll be around to take her off your hands," he suggested.

"And the Filipino—don't forget him." She turned back for her coat, shrugged into it and took a red knitted hood from the shelf. "I have a feeling," she said, tying the strings under her chin, "that this is going to be an uncomfortable kind of Christmas. Paula will have enough expensive gifts to start a store, and the poor Filipino will have so few that we'll be embarrassed by our own modest display. I'd kind of hoped for a normal one."

"Times change, chum," Lindsey answered philosophically, thinking pleasantly of Paula. "It might turn out to be fun."

"I hope so."

She let herself out into the night, walked along the porch to the side steps and driveway, wishing Christmas could be the way it always had been: Gramps and Gram coming for the tree and church and dinner, giggling conversations over the telephone about the wondrous gifts Santa Claus had brought, groups of girls touring from house to house, delivering and receiving more packages, and the record player going like crazy on the third floor from five o'clock on, with time out for cold turkey sandwiches and hot chocolate. For as long as she could remember, she had had such Christmases; first as a little girl carrying her doll to other little girls' houses, then, as she grew older, proudly displaying the evening dress which was a surprise only because it was more beautiful than she had imagined it could be.

This year, Paula would come with a dozen evening dresses; and Jinx's pleasure in owning his own tuxedo, instead of a hand-me-down, would be spoiled because the guest from Bangkok, or wherever he hailed from, would be homesick and envious.

"He might even be a heathen," she said aloud, starting to slide.

The air was bracing, the long driveway slanted down to the street. With a running start on the ruts that cars had made, she sailed along, arms outspread, and felt as if she were flying. A leap at the sidewalk landed her against a tree, and she clung there, laughing. If the snow lasted, nothing could ruin Christmas! But would it last? Snow had a discouraging habit of melting quickly in New Jersey.

Oh, well, she thought, trudging through white drifts instead of walking on the neatly cleaned sidewalk, it was hers to enjoy tonight. No one could see how silly she acted; and if she wanted to, she could lie right down on the Mason's terraced lawn, rub her arms up and down, and make an angel. She lay down and made one, then moved on and made two more. Snow tickled under her collar, so she shook herself, pranced a bit, and wished she had brought Blair's sled. Running and coasting would have been fun, all the way to the last corner where the neon lights began. She thought of going back for it, then decided to skip along the sidewalk for a while, instead.

When she finally reached the drugstore, red-cheeked and puffing, its only customer was a boy who was in one of her classes at school. He looked up from the magazine he was reading and offered a casual, "Hi." She returned it, just as casually, then went back to lean on the counter while old Mr. Peterson took her ointment from a shelf and wrapped it in blue paper.

The boy's name was Paul. Paul—what? she wondered. Benton? Banning? Yes, that was it, Banning. Paul Banning. He lived out in the country somewhere, and Jinx had said he stayed with his grandparents during the week, in one of the big houses on Cedar Lane.

She took her package, said, "Thanks, Mr. Peterson, just charge it, please," and was about to start another joyous journey home when Paul left the magazine rack and held the door open for her.

"Mind if I walk along with you?" he asked.

"Of course not."

She did mind, in a way, for she had planned to slip and slide again. Had he been Page Vandergren, she would gladly have fallen into a leisurely stroll, the more leisurely the better; but he wasn't. He was nice enough looking; strong-featured, blond, polite, but she didn't know him. She wasn't exactly sure of his name or where he lived. So she bobbed along and let him match his stride to hers while she cast about for something to say.

"Our cook burned her hand," she finally hit upon, "so I had to come for more medicine."

"Gee, that's a shame."

"It is, when you think of its happening to poor Stella," she answered. "Things are always happening to her."

"What sort of things?" He turned an interested, hatless head, and they had a topic.

"Oh, getting her feelings hurt and clobbering her thumb with a hammer when she should have let Jinx put up a shelf, things like that." Cinda was never at a loss for words for very long at a time; and, since Paul was a good listener, she chattered along freely, and even tacked on her own opinion of the unfortunate Stella. "She always makes me think of a poor little bird," she said, "hopping around on the fringe of things and nipping up the crumbs of other people's good times."

"Say, that's good!" Paul stopped to face her, and under the street lamp his eyes held surprised interest. "You ought to put that in one of your themes for Miss Alexander," he said.

Returning his gaze, Cinda thought of another comparison. He looked like an Indian standing there, a straight, tall Indian with light hair. His cheekbones were high and pronounced, his nose was high-bridged, and he held himself as if he had stopped on a forest path and were listening to sounds she couldn't hear. She wondered why she had never really noticed him before, and if working on a farm had made him stand so straight. "I'll try to remember it," she said, with her mind on something else. And she asked, "Don't you live on a farm?"

"A kind of farm," he answered, moving on again. "My father goes in for blooded cattle. I stay with my grandparents most of the week, though."

"I remember Jinx' telling me that. It seems to me he said—now what did he say?" Cinda liked to know as much as possible about her acquaintances, so she searched her memory for a remark Lindsey had once made about Paul Banning. "Oh, yes," she recalled happily, "last year he said that you came out for football and would have made the team, except that you always had to go home on Fridays. He said the coach tried to talk you into staying over."

"I didn't try out very long."

Paul looked more like an Indian than ever as he stalked along. "Stiff as a ramrod," was the way Cinda expressed it to herself, wondering what she had said to make him look so grim. But suddenly he put his hands in the pockets of his short coat and said simply, "My folks can't see any sense in my staying in town over week ends. They need me at home, and my grandmother backs them up. I'm probably a lot of trouble to her."

"For goodness' sake, why?"

She took a couple of quick steps to keep up with him. It seemed to her that anyone who lived on Cedar Lane would have enough servants to keep one extra person from being any trouble, but he gave a rueful shrug and said, "I suppose grandparents hate to start all over after they've raised their own children. Isn't this where you live?"

"Yes." She looked at the lighted windows far back on a white lawn, at the fat cupola standing out against the stars, at snow-laden shrubbery caressing the bulging porch, and said proudly, "This is my house. Won't you come in?"

"I'd better not."

"Jinx is upstairs, and he'd be glad of an excuse to stop studying," she urged; but he shook his head.

"No, thanks," he answered shortly. "It was swell of you to let me walk along with you. I'll see you in school tomorrow."

He was nice. He was no Page Vandergren, she thought, but he was ruggedly nice, and kind of sweet and shy. Impulsively she thrust out her mittened hand, and said as he grasped it, "I'll see you there, Paul."

"Right. English Lit. Third chair on the outside aisle."

She ran up the driveway; and when she turned to look around, he was still standing on the sidewalk. "If by any chance you're here on Friday night," she called, "come over. War-Horse will be home by then and we'll be having a gang in. We'd love to have you."

"I'm sure I won't be here, but thanks, anyway." He waved, and she waggled her mitten in return.

Queer, she thought, taking off her coat and boots in the hall closet, how many people there are in the world that you never get to know. How many *nice* people!

Her mother and father were playing Scrabble in the library, so she stopped beside them and announced, "I made a new friend tonight. He goes to my high school and I'm going to coax him over sometime. He's nice."

Then she went on to replace Stella's bandage with a fresh one.

Chapter III

CINDA snatched up her school books and hurried off to meet Kitty Lou at the corner. Everything had delayed her, from helping Stella with breakfast to running out in the snow and wresting her fountain pen from Bobo, who protested innocence even while she searched him; and then waiting just a few minutes to hear the result of another call from Colorado Springs.

Kitty Lou was usually the late one; but there she sat on a fire hydrant, looking cold and cross. Her name suited her so exactly: Kitty Lou Chappell. It suggested blonde curls, big blue eyes, and, when she remembered to use it, a soft, Southern accent. Kitty Lou had never been south of Washington, D.C., but her mother had been "bawn and raised in Gawgia," so from constant association with a legitimate drawl, hers was only a very slight affectation.

"Well, I do declare," she called as Cinda panted up, "I'm almost frozen to this seat. What made you so late?"

"Millions of things," Cinda puffed. "It was a perfectly foul morning. Our cook burned her hand and my cousin's coming to visit. Paula Marsh. You know her—the far-distant cousin from Colorado? And War-Horse is bringing home a guest, and Moth's moving everybody around—just as if it all had to be planned right this minute. When I left, she had decided to put Bobo on the couch in the sewing room and give his room to the Filipino."

"The *who?*"

"The guy War-Horse is bringing home."

As they crossed the street, Cinda launched into an account of what little she knew of their strange guest. Kitty Lou listened, frowning, and said glumly at the end, "He won't be any good to us. And if we don't want him for parties, we won't get Warren, either. I don't see why he had to invite him."

"Pooh," Cinda retorted practically, "War-Horse never gangs around with us. He's *twenty!* Oh, he shows up at the Country Club Junior Party, but he never asks you to dance, and you know it."

"He might." Kitty Lou tossed her blue hood with little bells on it, and said complacently, "I'm oldah, now. I'm out of the sub-deb class. I'm moah sophisticated."

"Did you get the kind of formal you wanted?" Cinda shifted her books and was eager to learn what luck someone else might have had with a brief, boned bodice above a long, full skirt.

But Kitty Lou sighed and said with a flat, northern twang, "No, darn it. Mother just sat there and looked shocked. Every time Miss Hattie brought out a really decent dress, she shrieked, 'Oh, Hattie, take it *away!* This is for a *child,* remember. Bring something with a square neck.' A *square neck! Imagine!*"

"What did you buy?"

"I don't know. It's yellow. It's net. And I will say for it, it hasn't much back in it—just enough to curve up and meet the front and hook onto *great—wide*—straps."

Kitty Lou had been secretly delighted with the dress, because it was far more revealing than she had dared hope; but, having bragged that she would hold out for one with only enough top to curve dramatically above her small bosom, she had to discredit it. "It'll do, I guess," she said. "But, *oh, Cinda!*" She stopped so suddenly on the sidewalk that a group of hurrying girls bumped into her. "I saw *Page*!" she cried, staring past Cinda with her mouth a little open, just as if he had reappeared before her. Then she pulled herself back from the vision to breathe, "We were coming out of the dress shop as he drove by. It was bitter cold but he had the top down, and there he was—looking straight at me. In that dreamy Sunbeam Talbot. He grinned and . . . " She tramped on again and said wrathfully, "There was Mother, too; carrying the dress box, and wearing boots and that horrible old fur coat that's about six inches shorter than her skirt! And right at that minute, just as he was sort of turning in to the curb, what did she do but reach out and take hold of my arm—exactly as if she wanted him to be sure and know we were together. Of course he went on, and I was so embarrassed I wanted to die!"

Cinda laughed. The chances were about a thousand to one that Page would have offered Kitty Lou a lift home, even had her mother been wearing her new Persian lamb coat and the hat that Kitty Lou said she had paid fifty-five dollars for, or even had she vanished in thin air. When any girl rode beside Page Vandergren in his low-slung sports car, it was Melody Ayer. Cinda had been in it once, squashed into the bucket seat on Lindsey's lap, and Kitty Lou had got no nearer than to lean against a front fender while Page was in the movie theater.

"I wouldn't worry," she said. "Melody will be home from boarding school next week, and just one little ride wouldn't do you much good."

"He might have found out that I'm a lot cuter than Melody." Kitty Lou's smile and toss of her head were confident, but she said frankly, "Lucky you. At least he comes to your house with Jinx."

There was no rivalry between the two. Partly because Page merely said, "Hi, there," to each one impartially, and partly because Cinda always notified Kitty Lou when Lindsey brought him home. Sometimes Cinda wondered if Kitty Lou would be as fair, or if the fun of watching for Page, going where he might be, suffering volubly together, yearning and giggling over him, wasn't the greater part of his attraction for them. He was good-looking, she had to admit that, and he had a father who was president of a television corporation in New York, and he lived in one of the fine houses on Cedar Lane. And he had a long, low, yellow car. He also had a girl—Melody Ayer. They were going steady.

"He pulled open my locker door last week, when it stuck," Kitty Lou reported for the third time. "And he said . . . " She broke off to clasp her books again and drawl in an awed voice, "My goodness, Cinda, theah he is!"

The yellow car was pulling into the parking lot beside the school. Page sat alone behind the wheel, swinging into a vacant space behind a large orange bus that had stopped to unload its student passengers. Cinda watched a group scatter from a snow storm his tires spun back and found herself saying with a shock of disappointment, "Oh, it was mean of him to come so close. He was showing off."

"I thought it was cute." Kitty Lou began to hurry a little, tossing her head so that the little bells on her cap jingled merrily, and smiling as if she and Cinda were having an animated and amusing conversation. "Well, deah me," she laughed, although Cinda had said nothing at all.

Cinda walked silently beside her, wishing Page had parked the way the next car was doing, slowly, and waiting for people to get out of its way. And when Kitty Lou hissed, "*Say* something! Don't just *stare*!" she answered, "Paul Banning walked home from the drugstore with me last night."

"That lug?" Kitty Lou forgot to appear gay, and gave Cinda an incredulous stare. "That horrible lug?" she asked again, as they turned onto the walk leading to the long brick school. "Mercy, didn't you almost die?"

"I liked him." Cinda watched Lindsey's gang crawl out of the sedan beside Page's low-slung monster and said seriously, "I thought he was nice, Kit."

"He's utterly, utterly repulsive," Kitty Lou declared, ringing her bells again to express revulsion. "He never smiles, and he isn't even polite, and he's a—he always keeps his big old nose stuck in a book. He makes me think of the great, stone Sphinx —or something."

"How do you know so much about him?" Cinda asked curiously. "You've never even talked to him."

"I did, once." Kitty Lou blushed faintly, for she had failed to mention a morning last year, just after Paul Banning had transferred to the Glenvale high school. He was a new boy; and her mother had said his grandparents were "those aristocratic Bannings out on Cedah Lane, rich as cream but awfully queah and stand-offish." So she had accosted him in the hall and fluttered her lashes at him. Her temperamental locker was a great help at times, but it hadn't been that morning. Paul Banning had opened its door, said, "There you are," and gone on while she was still looking up at him with her eyes blinking. And when she had tried to thank him, later, he had mumbled curtly, "Forget it," and walked away again.

"My mothah says," she disclosed importantly, "that he hasn't a speck of get-up-and-go to him. His fathah makes him work like a dog all Saturday and Sunday, and his grandmothah keeps him shut up in that big house all durin' the week. And he minds them, too. How," she asked, "did he evah get to stay out late enough fo' you to meet him in the drugstoah?"

"I don't know. He was in there. And he didn't seem in much of a hurry as we walked along."

Cinda went up the steps and waved at girls she knew. Giggly little Marty O'Conner pulled her inside the hall as if they hadn't met for days, launching into a complete resumé of a movie she had seen the night before, until Barbie Devereaux drew Kitty Lou into the group and whispered to the three of them, "Don't tell anybody, but a garage mechanic told my father that Mary Spillman—that lush blonde in Jinx's home room—eloped last night. They've had all the state police out and are trying to get her back and have it annulled! Isn't it exciting?"

Other groups were in huddled conversation, too. No one moved in the wide foyer, so it was evident that Mary Spillman had provided quite a zip to the morning. Cinda didn't know her, could scarcely remember how the girl looked, but she hoped romantically, along with the others, that Mary and her groom had eluded their pursuers and would get away on a honeymoon. The fact that the young husband had just been drafted into the army made it even more imperative that they have a few days of happiness before he was dragged away to camp.

Cinda knew her mother would shake her head and say, "Oh, the foolish children." And hanging away her coat, she thought it, too. Even with no war on, she considered rationally, it wouldn't be any fun to be married to a soldier who was off somewhere where you couldn't go. Or even to a boy who stayed home and had no steady job. Barbie had said that the boy Mary Spillman had run off to marry was glad to be drafted, because he had no job.

"Mrs. Hollister, you needn't worry about your daughter's ever doing it," she mumbled, stooping over to pick up her books. Then she walked up the ramp to her home room, where her first class would be held.

Paul came in just after she had put her books in her desk and found the day's assignment in *Hamlet*. She had watched eagerly for him; and she grinned at him above the bent heads between them. He grinned back, hesitantly at first, until she sent him a little nod and a comradely wink. Then his grin widened, and he laid his volume of Shakespeare face-down on the arm of his chair. As a senior, with a junior credit to make up, he sat off to one side with two other students; and when he had his book in place, his notebook on top of it, he took a pencil from his pocket and ambled across the room to the pencil sharpener on the outside wall.

It would have been nearer to have gone around by the front desks and past the teacher's platform, but he chose the back way; and as he reached Cinda's aisle, he dropped his pencil. He stood watching it roll along the aisle, much as a football player guards his teammate's punt and lets it roll as far as it will; and when it finally came to rest beside Cinda's chair, he made a dive for it.

"Sorry," he said, retrieving it and leaving a folded note in her lap.

Cinda thought the note would scorch a hole in her navy blue skirt. Miss Alexander was not enough dazzled by her coming marriage to be blind to any bit of byplay in her classroom; and she only turned her gaze away because it was Paul who scrambled along the aisle. Paul never passed notes to girls.

Cinda felt for the piece of paper, heard it crackle when she tried to unfold it, and jerked her fingers away so quickly that she dropped it. Now it was her turn to lose a pencil; and she managed to knock her notebook off, too, and slip the note inside it. Then the class was called to order, and Kitty Lou had stumbled halfway through a soliloquy that would have put both Shakespeare and Hamlet to shame, before she had a chance to read what Paul had written.

I enjoyed last night, he had penned carefully. *Do you like to walk along a country road in the snow? Perhaps building a fire and roasting hot dogs over the flames? Or buying cheese and crackers in a crossroad store that smells of peppermint sticks and fresh-cut Christmas greens?*

That was all there was. Cinda read the words twice without looking up before she tore a page from her own notebook. She knew what Paul meant, so she scrawled, *I love to. When?* Then she folded the paper into a small, compact wad and listened attentively to the really interesting way Miss Alexander took over and explained the tortured mind of Hamlet.

Giving the note to Paul was easy. They reached the door at the same time, bumped shoulders, touched hands, and the deed was done. Cinda had only to wonder on what afternoon she was going for a snowy tramp, and what excuse she would give her three best friends for not showing up in the dingy café across the street.

I'll simply tell Kitty Lou the truth, she practiced, knowing she couldn't keep it from her, anyway. I'll say, "You may not like him, but I do. I feel sorry for him and I like him, so don't go getting ideas." I'll tell her right after school.

But after school she and Paul were striking off across back lots to her house.

"I'll stop by and tell Mother," she had said, when she had found him standing beside her locker. "I'll need my old snow suit and boots."

And she had hustled him out the side door and across people's yards, explaining in her voluble way, "It isn't that I'm trying to sneak out on the girls or trying to keep them from knowing. It's just that they'd think it's so utterly . . . " She stopped and amended, "They'd never understand why anyone should want to go *walking* when she might get a chance to ride around in somebody's car. Barbie never walks six feet if she can help it."

"I don't have a car," Paul said, holding up a clothesline for her to duck under.

"Pooh, who cares! I don't have one, either," she returned, "and Jinx wouldn't, except that Gramps is such a good, kind soul. Nobody but Jinx could keep Gramp's old hunting car running. If we cut through here we'll come out right across the street from my house."

She hurried him along the porch, rushed ahead to hospitably throw open the door, and called from inside the hall, "Moth, are you home?"

"In the library, darling."

"I want you to meet someone."

Mrs. Hollister came through the living room holding her knitting, her ball of yarn trailing behind her; and Cinda put her red mitten on Paul's arm as she said proudly, "This is my new friend, Paul Banning."

"How do you do, Mrs. Hollister?" Paul shook hands with Cinda's mother and a mixture of needles and knitting, then bent down to retrieve the ball of yarn. "It was swell of Cinda to bring me home with her," he said, rewinding. "There you are."

He held out the red ball; and she accepted it with a smile, saying, "Thank you, Paul. I know your grandparents very slightly, and your mother and I served together on a garden club committee a number of years ago. How is she?"

"She's—just fine."

Something seemed to close in his face. Perhaps it was the way his lips bit together then jerked into a smile, or the blank politeness in his eyes; but it made her ask quickly, "What are you two planning to do this afternoon?"

"We're going for a long walk," Cinda announced with enthusiasm. "Imagine anyone but Paul and me liking to mush along in the snow! We're going for a walk in the country and eat cheese and crackers in a grocery store!"

"Oh, honey, I don't know." Mrs. Hollister hated to sound motherly and unreasonably anxious, but she had to remind, "There are so many cars on the highways, and so much snow and ice."

"We'd planned to follow a little country road I know," Paul put in quickly. "It circles around past some houses but nobody uses it much. The corner store still has a wood-burning stove and a pickle barrel, right out in the middle, but if you'd rather we wouldn't . . . "

"It sounds like fun," she said, giving in, "so don't waste any time. I'd like to go, myself."

"We'd like to take you along."

He grinned at the eager sparkle in her eyes, but she laughed and said, "We only have one snow suit large enough to fit me, and from the puffing and panting I hear, Cinda has it halfway on. Bring Warren's old galoshes for Paul, dear," she called. "And an extra muffler and the cap with ear flaps."

Paul thought of saying that he never wore a hat, but Cinda had stuffed her skirt into her baggy pants and was pitching things at him from the closet, and her mother was as interested in getting them into their outfits as if they were starting off on an Arctic expedition.

"Have fun!" she cried, as they clumped out the door. "And if you see any good Christmas trees for sale, let me know."

She stood at the window, watching; and Cinda turned around to wave. Paul waved, too, and said as they went on, "She's swell. You don't think she'll worry, do you?"

"Nope. Not after she once makes up her mind. She's a terrific worrier until she finally decides a question. After that . . . " She waved her arms and hurried him along so they could reach the street that led to the street that led to the lane he knew.

She felt as if she had known Paul a long, long time. They talked about school as they walked in sparkling stillness; they talked about how hot they were with the heavy mufflers binding their necks, and, conspirators in treachery, they stopped and took them off. Cinda tied hers through the belt of her blue suit and let it hang like a plaid banner, its fringe dragging little tracks in the whipped cream snow. And finally they climbed across a ditch and sat down on the white bank of a field to rest.

"Just listen to how still it is." Cinda crossed her arms on her knees and said, sniffing, "And smell the wood smoke. Except for that house over behind those trees, we could be a million miles from anywhere. I think I'd like to live in the country." There was no answer, so she turned her head and asked, "Don't you like it?"

"No."

He had his Indian look on again; staring off into space, his face expressionless. He looked so like a carved and painted statue that she wondered why he had wanted to walk around in the country, when he said he didn't like it. For Cinda to wonder was to ask.

"Gracious me, Paul," she cried, "you're *in it!* Why would you want to bring me out here, and then look so mad?"

"I'm not mad." He turned and suddenly smiled at her, and she could see the little muscles along his jaw twitch. "I'm kind of a grouchy fellow," he said. "Come on, let's push on to the store. That relic of a stove's worth seeing, and so are the old guys who sit around it."

"Paul." She had no intention of moving, even if she froze solid in the snow. No one could be as companionable as Paul was one minute, then so unreachable the next, unless he had some deep-rooted bitterness in his heart. Twice, she thought, he's clammed up: last night when I invited him in, and just now when I mentioned living in the country. "What's wrong?" she asked bluntly. "If we're going to be friends I think you ought to tell me. We are friends, aren't we, Paul?"

"I hope so, Cinda."

"Then . . . " He was still smiling but she shook her head at him. "I don't think so," she said. "Friends tell each other worrisome things. Of course," she admitted, hunching up her shoulders, "I don't have much to tell, but—if I ever should—I'd tell you. Jinx," she explained hopefully, "is a pretty good friend of mine. I asked him some questions about myself yesterday, and he straightened me out. That's why people want to have friends instead of just acquaintances. I guess," she sighed, "if you're just an acquaintance, we might as well go on."

"Cinda, listen." He took off his heavy cap, brushed his hair back with the sleeve of his jacket, and sat turning the cap in his hands as he said soberly, "I'm slower at making friends than you are, or maybe I don't have the right approach. I thought you were a pretty girl, that's all. I've watched you go off in cars with a gang, laughing and having fun, and I wondered how the heck I could ever get a date with you."

"Why, you could have called me up and asked me for one!" she cried. "Any time!"

"I thought, last night," he went on, as if he hadn't heard her, "that now was my chance to do it. I could walk home with you and suggest going to a movie. And then I realized that it would keep me out too late—and I couldn't. I hated myself for being such a crumb. I hated myself even more for writing you a note and asking you for a date in the middle of the afternoon. In the middle of the afternoon," he repeated bitterly. "I wasn't thinking about being friends, that's straight, Cinda. I was only being brave and asking you, or someone, for a date."

"Oh," she said in a small voice.

"I . . . " He hesitated before he told her honestly, "Perhaps if Kitty Lou had been the one to come in the drugstore, I'd have latched onto her. I don't know. I wouldn't have suggested a walk today, though, I do know that, because I wouldn't be able to talk to her. I guess I shouldn't have suggested it to you, either."

"Yes, you should, Paul." Cinda put out her mitten and gave his knee a little pat; then she crossed her arms again and said gently, "I don't quite understand what it is you're trying to prove to yourself. I didn't know that boys ever worry about asking girls for dates. Jinx and War-Horse don't. They get turned down sometimes, but they don't worry about it. They just ask someone else."

"O.K." He sat up straight and faced her. "You've been prodding me, so here it is. Your brothers don't have parents like mine. They don't have grandparents like mine. They're well-adjusted kids. They can play football and go out at night without having the book thrown at them. They have something besides study, study, study, work, work, work, in their lives. They don't have a father who thinks money is the most important thing in life—far more important than his wife and son; they don't have a grandmother who's afraid of drafts and burglars, who keeps all her doors locked, and then double-bolts them as soon as the servants leave. And they don't have a mother who cries a lot of the time."

"Oh, Paul, I'm so sorry."

"They don't have to live with crumbling old age five days out of the week," he poured out, as if a dam had burst and released a torrent of misery, "then go home to a lousy week end. Do you know what we have in my grandparents' house?" he asked, staring at her, then dropping his head again. "We have a ballroom with crystal chandeliers and gold chairs around the walls. And do you know what we have in the country? We have a swimming pool and a gone-to-pieces tennis court. Nobody dances or swims or plays tennis in the houses I live in. Nobody in Glenvale is good enough to come to a dance—they might steal the heirlooms—and to keep a swimming pool filled and repaired is a waste of time and money. I have crackpots for grandparents and a crackpot of a father, who's getting more like them every day of his life."

"But your mother," Cinda put in timidly. "Surely she . . ."

"I sweat it out because of Mother," he interrupted. "Father kept at her until she gave up her garden club and any other outside activity she enjoyed, and she developed some sort of a nervous twitch and has spells of depression. I can pull her out of them when I'm around—but I don't think I can do it much longer."

"You'll be going away to college," she reminded him timidly, hoping the thought of next year's release would cheer him.

"I don't know." He hung his hands between his knees and sat contemplating his big gloves, as he said, "I wanted to go to Lawrenceville last year, so I could prep faster for Princeton, and you'd have thought I'd asked for a gold-plated hot-rod. It cost *money!* Driving from home to the nearest accredited high school every day would cost money, too, so that was out. Even my father had to admit that the high school nearest to us was no good, but he had to figure out in dollars and cents how much *money* he'd lose if I wasn't around to help, mornings and evenings. Free board at my grandparents' made up for the cost of hiring a man in my place, so I moved in to Glenvale. I'll either have to get a scholarship somewhere, next year, or go off and join the army."

"Oh, Paul, you wouldn't do *that*!" Cinda burst out. "Enlist, I mean. Why, with the grades you get, you're sure to have a scholarship."

"I haven't decided. I'll be eighteen in a couple of weeks, so I could do my hitch and go to school on my GI Bill of Rights. I could save my pay and be independent by then."

She was heartsick for this boy who should be looking confidently toward a future in college, with all the lovely, kind things wealthy parents could give him. She wanted to say something comforting, just the right thing, but no words came to her. It was impossible to coax him cheerily, as she would have Lindsey, "Oh, cheer up, pal, everything will be all right tomorrow." Dozens of tomorrows had put Lindsey back on top of the world; but unless a miracle happened, Paul Banning would find tomorrow exactly the same as today.

She was so quiet that he misunderstood her silence. "Well, that's the way it is," he looked around to say with light finality, "so let's forget it. I dragged it out when I knew I shouldn't, and I'm sorry. Come on, let's take a look at that grocery store."

He got up, slid down the bank and reached up to her, but she sat looking at him. "Paul," she said thoughtfully, "it's going to be better. It has to be. You told me about it, and that has to help

—a little. And you can come to our house—we don't care whether it's at night or in the daytime—and play table tennis and shuffleboard. There's always a crowd around."

"Sure, Cinda."

"Being with other people keeps anybody from being lonesome and feeling alone," she persisted, studying his expression and hoping the pitiful little crumbs of comfort she offered would be enough for one meal, until she could condition him to a wholesome diet of Hollisters.

"Sure. I feel fine, now. I feel really good."

She regarded him doubtfully, feeling that she had failed to find the right words; then she put her hand in his and slid down to stand beside him. "If my mother telephones your grandmother would you stay and have dinner with us?" she asked.

"I'll see. Thanks, though."

It would be folly to tell her that at five-forty-five, on the dot, he would follow his grandparents into the massively furnished dining room and have a cup of clear soup placed before him. At six-o-five the silent meal would end with tapioca pudding or a spongy desert, at six-ten he would check all the windows, and at six-twenty-five he would let the elderly servants out the back door, leave the light on until they reached their apartment above the garage, then double bolt the door behind them. It was nightly custom, but Cinda would never understand it.

"We could get in a couple of sets of table tennis before dinner," she was saying eagerly, "if Stella's hand's all right, that is. If it isn't, you could help me set the table. We're never very formal with guests. I guess we can't be," she laughed, trying to make conversation as they walked along, "because we have so many of them. There's always somebody popping in for a meal or to spend the night, and Mother never knows how many she's going to feed."

It suddenly occurred to her that praising her family's hospitality might, following on the heels of his complaint, sound like bragging. "I–I mean," she stammered, "well–there are such a lot of us, you know, and–and if each one invited a guest at the same time it would throw Moth into a fit."

"I liked your mother."

"You did? I'm glad. Moth," she declared with great confidence, "will have your grandmother practically begging us to have you over often. She works for the Blood Bank when we have a drive on, and Daddy says she can talk a person into giving away his last red corpuscle."

They turned a bend in the lane and saw a small country store beside an intersection of what once might have been two well-traveled roads. It had three steps leading up to a sagging front porch that made an ideal vantage spot for the proprietor, when he wished to sit and scan the countryside, and offered shelter to pedestrians who were caught in a shower. A long sign above the porch, blurred by years of weathering, proclaimed GENERAL MERCHANDISE–WILLIS WISE, PROP. The whole structure needed a coat of paint, but two windows on each side of its center door shone like bright eyes in an old, weather-beaten face.

"Hi, Mr. Wise," Paul said, opening the ancient door carefully and following Cinda inside.

"Howdy, boy. Haven't seen you around for a few days."

An old man leaned on the glass top of a case filled with odds and ends of small kitchen equipment, everything from pot-holders to sieves and meat grinders; and two other old men, who sat before a round, fat, redly-glowing stove, let down the front legs on their splint-bottomed chairs to look around.

"Well, if it ain't our young orator," one said, grinning and taking his heavy work shoes from the iron rail around the stove, and smoothing down his sparse hair that still stood up from following a cap he had pulled off over three hours before. "You come back to finish that argument about the President runnin' for a second term?" he asked.

"No, sir, not today." Paul drew Cinda nearer to his three old cronies, then said, as proudly as she had when she had introduced him to her mother, "I brought my friend to meet you. This is Cinda Hollister."

Chapter IV

AFTER the long walk and in spite of Mrs. Hollister's persuasiveness, Paul had put on his heavy jacket and was saying goodby to Cinda at the door. His grandmother had been charming but firm, and Cinda had heard her mother say, "We'll hope to have him stay some other time, then," and put down the telephone.

"It's not fair!" she burst out, slamming the door after Paul and flying back into the library. "That old witch makes me furious!"

"Cinda!" Her mother looked up from the knitting she was trying to unravel, sighed, "Oh, I'll never finish this by Christmas," and admonished in the same breath, "honey, that was a very disrespectful way to talk. Paul probably didn't really want to stay, and he and his grandmother had their signals, just as you and Lindsey and I do. If Lindsey had wanted to stay, he'd have grabbed the phone and said, 'Lay off, Mom.' "

"But you don't understand." Cinda opened her mouth to explain the strange relationship between Paul and his family, then closed it again. Paul had talked to her in confidence. He had said on the way home, "You're the only person I've ever beefed to, Cinda. Please don't tell anyone."

And now she was about to pull out his affairs, just as if she were opening a dresser drawer for her mother to examine its contents. She wanted very much to have her mother look them over and put them in better order, but it wouldn't be fair. "I guess you're right," she said with a sigh. "Perhaps we can invite him some other time."

She went slowly up the stairs and stopped to look at Down Boy. who was taking a nap on the window seat below the stained glass window. He jumped up to lick her face when she leaned across him to select a large blue stone, rub it and make a wish, then he hopped off the thick gray cushion and padded along behind her. They found Lindsey in his room, putting his closet back the way it had been that morning.

"I am not moving into Bobo's little room, so Bobo can move into the sewing room, so Cousin Maud can sleep in here," he announced flatly, hanging a sports jacket on the rod and looping a pair of old cords over a hook. "You get to stay where you are, and I have my rights."

"I'll have Paula rooming with me," she pointed out.

"That's O.K. You like her. Buff can turn out for Cousin Maud." He thumped a pair of shoes onto the shelf, then looked around to ask, "Didn't I see you and Paul Banning tripping up the driveway together?"

"We had an afternoon date."

"Well, gosh all hemlock!" He hung a tie rack on the closet door, and said, while he carefully arranged his flamboyant collection of bright silks over it, "You looked like Ichabod Crane and a lady midget. Don't tell me he parted with enough cash for a couple of cokes."

Cinda forgot how much she had liked Lindsey only yesterday afternoon. She stood in the middle of the doorway and snapped, "I think you're being utterly—*and I do mean utterly*—horrid! What right have you to say nasty things about Paul Banning when he had nothing but praise for you? He talked wonderfully about you, and he envied you—and—and now you make fun of him!"

"Wups, hold it. I didn't make fun of him," Lindsey answered, walking over to the bed and picking up a pile of undershirts and shorts. "I just said . . ."

"You did! You did make fun of him." Tears came into Cinda's eyes and she stamped her foot. "You did, you did, you did!" Each time her shoe slapped the bare floor Down Boy leaped against her. He thought they were playing a new game, and she had to push him off. "Oh, *keep down!*" she wailed.

"Well, holy cats." Lindsey dumped his pile of underclothes back on the bed and gave her his full attention. Cinda seldom went off on a temperamental binge, but she was in the middle of a dandy right now, so he asked, "Are you nuts about him?"

"No!"

"Did he make passes at you?"

"Of *course*, not!"

How to make anyone so dense as Lindsey understand that Paul was a wonderful guy was beyond her—unless she spoke straight out and betrayed a confidence. And even then he was apt to ask, "Why the heck didn't he up and tell his grandmother he wanted to stay?" That question had been nagging at her, too, all the way upstairs. She liked Paul, she enjoyed him; but, and she had to face it, she was disappointed in him. So many emotions in one afternoon, so much pity and pull at her heartstrings, had made her lash out at Lindsey, who was quite innocent of any wrong. "Oh, darn it," she groaned. "I'm sorry."

"Think nothing of it."

"I'll help you put your stuff back in the dresser drawers."

"I'd rather do it, thanks." He sauntered across the room, whistling as if she weren't there, pulled open drawers and dropped underwear and socks inside. Then he sauntered back for a box of dress studs and cuff-links, the cummerbund he wore with a dinner jacket, and a pile of smooth, white shirts. "Goodness, are you still around?" he asked, noticing her against the doorframe.

"I don't ever seem to know what to do about anything," she answered dismally.

Her eyes still looked tear-drenched, so he tossed off a kind, "Oh, cheer up, kid, the teens are hard," and inspected the job a laundry had done on his shirts.

"I mean," Cinda ventured, coming inside and sitting down on the bed, "I don't think I'm very helpful to people. I don't know what to say to them—so I don't say anything."

"You said quite a piece a minute ago."

"But that was different. I was mad at you, and I wasn't trying to—to bolster your morale."

"Well, I should hope not." He shut the last drawer on his possessions which nestled in their rightful place again, and remarked, "That's that. Are you going to come down to dinner or stay up here and mope?"

"I wasn't moping, Jinx," she protested. "Truly, I wasn't. I was trying to ask you to be nice to Paul without telling you that he has a hard time at home and may do something rash." She stopped, clapped her hand over her mouth and mumbled through it, "I mean, I just want you to like him."

"I like him." He closed the closet door and said, "Mrs. Hollister had better not let me catch her in here again," then made an expansive gesture toward the hall. "After you, princess."

Cinda slid a reluctant inch forward. She had hoped for understanding and assistance from Lindsey; but it seemed that she could rarely depend on him to show good sense, and her time had been wasted. "If one has a problem," she tried once more, enigmatically, "and one tells someone else about it—in confidence—shouldn't one try to do something? That is, if one can?"

Lindsey regarded her very patiently before he spoke. "If I understood you correctly," he said finally, "the 'one' of the first part might not care to have the 'one' of the second part dip into the 'one' of the first part's business. And if you are the 'one' of the second part, the 'one' of the first part most definitely wouldn't. Does that answer your question?"

"Sort of."

She still sat, so he went on, "Let me remind you that you dipped into some of Buff's business, once, and the beautiful Charmion didn't speak to her for a week. And you helped Mom and the PTA to a slight altercation; and Dad's secretary thought she was about to quit her job and get married, all because you misinterpreted a few kind remarks Sammy Eglin made about her. Remember those times when you tried to 'do something?' "

"Yes," she admitted sadly, "but I was only thirteen, then. I ought to know how to meet a situation, now. I do want to so much, Jinx," she said, lifting troubled eyes to his. "But I don't seem to know how. You just don't understand."

"I'll give the matter my personal attention after the holidays," he answered, showing he did. "Sometimes I think I'm getting in a rut, running around with the same old gang. There're a lot of nice guys in high school we ought to ask over—especially ones from the country. Now get up and go down and see if Stella's still laid up, will you?"

"All right, Jinx. Thank you."

Cinda felt as if she had betrayed Paul. She dreaded to see him again, for she would have to confess her inadvertent slip, apologize for it, and minimize its importance as best she could. She hoped he would shrug it off as "nothing at all," but from the little she knew of him, he wasn't the shrugging-off type. So she worried about it all the way to school the next morning, even while Kitty Lou teased her about her "screamingly funny date," and wondered what was wrong with her that she never could keep a confidence, or a secret, or even her own affairs, to herself.

I just plain talk too much, she decided sadly, hanging her coat in her locker. I have to babble all the time and get other people to bolster me up and do my thinking for me. I'm absolutely undependable. She gave a discouraged sigh as she tossed her scarf on the shelf, and silently vowed, if Paul ever tells me anything more, wild horses won't drag it out of me. I'll confess everything right away, and from now on I'll be a regular rock for him to lean on.

But she had no opportunity either to confess or to turn herself into a rock. Paul sent her a friendly grin across the classroom, or said, "Hi, Cinda," when he met her in the halls; but he didn't ask her to go walking again. He passed right by without even stopping to talk. And the snow melted. In three days, the whole lovely, white town became slippery, dirty slush.

"It won't be a white Christmas," Mrs. Hollister lamented, late Friday afternoon, as she was pressing red ribbon in the service pantry while Cinda opened big cartons that held the holly wreaths. "Though why I should care I don't know. Warren has a long drive home this afternoon, and I'm glad the roads are clear, Stella?" she called. "Did I buy rice?"

"Enough to feed an army," Stella returned shortly, from the kitchen. "White, brown, wild. Take your choice."

"White tonight," Mrs. Hollister chose happily, testing her iron and looking down at Cinda, who was sucking a pricked thumb. "I haven't the least idea what Orientals eat, but I do know they like rice. I thought that chicken and rice would be safe for a starter. Do you think we should try chop suey tomorrow?"

"Search me." Cinda squeezed out a drop of blood, wiped it off on the carton, and reminded her mother, "War-Horse hates rice."

"But he has a guest who likes it. We must always remember to have tea with our meals, too, and put bamboo shoots in things. They don't taste too bad, and it may be fun to vary our diet. If your father fusses, we can feed him something extra in the kitchen."

She thought it interesting to have a foreigner visit them over the holidays, mingling his odd customs with theirs; and she went on with her expansive planning while Cinda tied bows and carried each finished wreath to its appointed spot for hanging.

One was laid on the table beside the front door, one on the floor beneath each of the living room's four long windows, three in the dining room, three in the library. It was quite dark outside. Cinda could hear Lindsey repairing the Christmas tree stand in the basement, talking to Buff and Bobo, and pleading with Down Boy; and she had just deposited her last wreath in its temporary resting spot when the front door burst open.

"Hello! Hey! *Hello!*" Warren shouted. "Here we are!"

Cinda shot out of the library as her mother tore in from the pantry, and feet charged up the basement stairs.

"Hi, everybody!" Warren cried, catching Mrs. Hollister in a hug that lifted her off the floor. "Folks, this is Dick."

Those of the Hollister family who hadn't quite reached the front ranks stopped where they were, and stared.

The young man who had closed the door and was standing before it was as blond as Warren. He had blue eyes, too, and an upturned, inquisitive nose. He might have been born in Glenvale, America, or in any town in Sweden. "Dick Marshall," Warren said. "Well, say something to him, Mom."

"Mercy," was all Mrs. Hollister could think of to say. Then she held out her hand and began to laugh. "We're awfully glad to have you, Dick," she managed to get out before her mirth exploded again. "We—we expected someone so different," she tried to explain.

"Yeah, a Filipino." Bobo was disappointed. This guest was no different from dozens Warren had brought home, so he offered a disinterested, "Hi," and returned to the basement.

"What made you think Dick would be a Filipino?" Warren asked.

"We didn't," Cinda answered, pushing past Buff who had begun to dispense her customary charm—a light kiss for Warren and a curtsy for the puzzled guest. "That is, we didn't know he was Dick. Moth thought you were bringing a native from Bangkok or the Philippines, she couldn't remember which. Naturally . . ."

"I get it." Warren whooped with laughter, and Dick Marshall grinned at them all.

"I really am from Bangkok," he said. "My father's over in Thailand on a mission, so I came back to the States to college, and it's too far to go home for Christmas."

"We're glad to have you here with us." Mrs. Hollister was

completely herself again, but she silently resolved to run upstairs and telephone her husband, and to change the rice to potatoes. "Take off your coats, while Lindsey and Bobo bring in the bags," she urged, knowing that Stella must be forewarned first of all. "Cinda, suppose you run out to the kitchen," she suggested meaningly. "I may have left the iron on."

"I'll go," Warren volunteered before Cinda could move from the spot to which she was rooted. "I've got to see my old girl, Stella. Yes, I know," he laughed. "I'll explain to her. Or maybe we ought to put on a show for her. Can you speak Thai, Dick?"

"Not much. I could mix what I know with some double-talk, I guess."

"Now, you boys behave." Mrs. Hollister gave Warren a little push, and said with amusement to Dick, "Stella is quite apt to burst into tears from relief. She's been in a complete panic over having a foreigner to cook for. Warren can prepare her, then you can meet her casually. She does better that way." And she called after Warren, "Are you hungry?"

"Did you ever know me not to be?"

He went into the narrow back hall, shoved the basement door to, and crossed the dining room to bang on the service pantry door and announce himself. Lindsey disappeared to act as baggage master; Mrs. Hollister stopped the second hospitable curtsy Buff was about to make by taking her firmly by the hand and leading her upstairs; and Cinda was left to escort the guest into the living room.

"We certainly are glad you turned out to be an American," she said chattily, dropping his smart tweed topcoat on the bench beside Warren's old trenchcoat, and leading the way in. "We were resigned to eating exotic food for the next ten days, and goodness only knows what Cousin Maud would have said to you. She's coming, too, you know, and she's an author, and Moth was scared to death that she might talk your arm off. And Paula has a finicky appetite, and she might have gone on a hunger strike. You'll like Paula, though," she added hastily. "She's beautiful. She's older than I am and won't bore you."

Dick looked about the charming room with its slip-covered furniture and plain gray carpeting, then at Cinda's bright face, and said with a grin, "I don't see how any of the Hollisters could bore me. You've made me feel so welcome. But, gee," he said uneasily, "Warren didn't tell me you had other guests coming."

"It's only Cousin Maud and Paula," Cinda laughed. "You're the one we've been all excited about. You've no idea," she chattered on, nudging him gently toward the library, "what a panic we were in! The kitchen is simply bulging with rice; and Buff hoped you'd wear a turban, and Moth was so worried about church and Christmas, for fear you'd be a Buddhist, you know. And Orientals are so polite to their parents that she was afraid you'd think we're terribly ill-mannered and disrespectful to ours—especially Bobo. He forgets to wash, and is never very courteous. Moth made him promise to do everything she told him to, even though he said it would ruin his whole vacation."

"And still she let Warren bring me."

He stopped in the archway as if he couldn't believe it; but she looked up at him and answered with candor, "Why, of course. That's what Christmas is for: to be kind and loving to someone who needs it. As Daddy pointed out to Bobo, when he moaned and groaned about it, it would be a poor sort of Christmas is everyone thought of nothing but the gifts he would get. I was a little discouraged, too," she admitted. Then she hunched her shoulders and said with a pleased smile, "Now we don't have to worry about it. You're just like the the rest of us, so it can be a house party. You—you won't feel homesick, will you?" she asked anxiously.

"I hope not," he answered, thinking she was cute and wanting to tease her. "But what if I should? What would you do about it?"

"I don't know."

Warren always argued that Cinda never knew when she was being teased, while Lindsey thought she did, but was smart enough not to show it. Dick was undecided, as she said gravely, "I think I would tell War-Horse to invite Melody Ayer over. Melody can take anybody's mind off anything. Of course, Paula can, too; but she's out of circulation because of Jinx—and, maybe, War-Horse. Melody . . . " She sighed heavily as she remembered the way Melody had walked off with her own secret love, then said brightly, "Yes, Melody's the cure. If you can lure her away from Page Vandergren, that is."

"Do you want me to?"

Dick had studied the different expressions that romped across Cinda's face, even while he noticed how big and softly brown her eyes were, how long her lashes, how pert her nose; but she fooled him by throwing back her head and laughing.

"Of course not," she said. "I was only helping you not to be homesick and was kind of mentioning, in an offhand way, that Jinx is crazy about Paula. He doesn't know I know it," she said, contrite for another slip when it was too late, but glad to have given the warning, "so don't tell him I said it."

"I won't. And I'll run out of the room whenever the beautiful Paula enters. But what can I do if she pursues me?" he asked. "I have terrific charm for girls."

Cinda took her turn at studying a new face. Dick's was the likable kind; not homely, not handsome—just likable and happy.

He wouldn't be homesick, and he wouldn't have all the girls in Glenvale panting beside their telephones while they waited for his call.

"I think you'd know exactly what to do in any situation," she said.

They were sitting comfortably in two large chairs when Warren flung open the door from the dining room. He carried a plate of sandwiches in one hand and dragged Stella with the other, while Down Boy kept up with him in a series of lunges and leaps.

"This is our jewel," he said. "Down, boy. I mean," he added, untangling his introduction and pointing with his plate, "this is Stella. Down Boy's the mutt. Oh, gosh!"

He broke off a piece of sandwich and held it down to the dog while Stella tremblingly put out the hand with the burn on it, took it back and substituted the other one as Dick sprang up to give it a vigorous shake. "Here, you idiot," Warren grumbled, watching Down Boy leave the floor and snap at the bread; then he finished what was left of the sandwich and held out the plate. "Have one. Dad will be here in a few minutes, and he's going to yell bloody murder if I haven't moved that car."

"Lindsey's putting them all away." Stella was amazed that she could utter a whole sentence to one who had actually crossed the Pacific Ocean. The most she had hoped to do, after she had found the guest to be of the English-speaking species, was to shove her cookie jar at him and answer his thanks with a timid bob of her head. Now she found herself murmuring as she backed out the door, "I'm very glad you came."

"Great old girl," Warren commented, setting his plate on an ottoman, then straightening up to listen. "Don't tell me that's *Dad* coming home," he said, with lifted eyebrows, as the front door quietly opened and closed. "The empty driveway must have thrown the old boy."

He heard his mother run down the stairway, calling happily as she came, "Oh, darling, I'm so glad you're home a little early." There was no hearty bellowing, "By all the gods," even though Warren listened eagerly for it. There was only a mild reply, followed by a silence that had to mean a kiss, so he said, "Dad's sure on his good behavior," and hustled out to pump his father's hand and clamp a loving arm around his shoulders.

Chapter V

THE Christmas holidays had begun, as Cinda said, "with a bang." After dinner, Warren and Lindsey dragged the Christmas tree in from the back porch, nailed it firmly to its wooden standard, then, with much hoisting and shoving, and with confusing directions from the sidelines, managed to set its thick trunk in a pail of water.

"We'll have to trim it tonight," Mrs. Hollister decided, looking up from the almost undecipherable list she was studying. "With Christmas falling on Sunday and Maud and Paula coming tomorrow, I'll have to shop tomorrow night until the stores close. I haven't bought a thing."

"Not even my new tuxedo?" Lindsey asked, down on his hands and knees. "When you know I've grown right out of Warren's old one?"

"Nope." She shook her head. "I'm buying a chair for your room."

A groan answered her; and Warren asked, "How about my camera?"

"No." Her head shook again.

"Or my sports jacket?" Another shake.

"Or a new set of golf clubs to replace the beat-up old set of Dad's I've been using?"

Her head was swinging like a pendulum, but it stopped when she said, "You'd lose the camera before you finished the first film, you have a clothes allowance, and you won't be playing golf at the shore this summer."

"O.K." Warren turned to Dick and said firmly, "In that case, we'll give the ancients exactly one hour of our valuable time; then we'll go out on the town, whether the tree's finished, or not. Suit you?"

"I kind of like it here," Dick answered.

He had been helping Bobo rearrange the sectional divan so that it went around a corner and left room for the television to be moved from behind the tree; and Bobo inquired through the green branches, "Don't I get my autoharp, Mom?"

"You get a blue serge suit."

The telephone rang, and she absent-mindedly reached out for the receiver, answered, and passed it on to her husband. "For you, dear," she said, and went back to reviewing her list.

Cinda, who had been going in and out for the cartons of ornaments, had heard parts of the conversation, so she said with resignation, "Oh, well, I don't mind giving up my formal. It's nothing but a long dress, anyway, and never much of a surprise." And she added in a loud aside to Dick, "We're always supposed to suffer this way until Christmas morning." But Buff looked stricken.

"I had so hoped for a new doll," she sighed, showing such grief over the loss of motherhood that none could doubt her sincerity. "And a larger bike. But if you think I need something useful, Mother, dear, I'll try to bear it."

She crossed her arms on her little chest in a gesture of resignation, then cupped her hands and lifted them to her mouth in what she thought was a beautiful attitude of supplication.

"Is she supposed to be drinking from the poisoned cup or sucking an orange?" Lindsey asked, ruining her scene and making everyone laugh so hard that his father pleaded:

"Quiet, kids." Then he said, "All right, I'll be there;" and put the telephone down with a sigh of resignation.

"I don't know how you expected me to hear whether Jim Purcell is taking off for New York or Florida," he grumbled. "It's a fine thing when a man can't hear what his own partner says above the gabbling of his family. Well, let's get organized. Jinx, you bring the kitchen stepladder; Cinda, you can hand me things; Warren, you pass along the lights and connect them up when I'm ready. Buff and Bobo, you stay out of the way until we get to the lower branches." Mention of the bottom half of the tree reminded him of something, and he asked, "Where's that infernal dog?"

"Stella took him over to her sister's," Cinda answered, opening her boxes of ornaments and passing one, and a handful of wire hooks, to her mother.

"That's a break." Donald Hollister enjoyed decorating the tree more than anyone else in the family. When the children had been small, he had liked to look down from his ladder at their shining faces; now he liked to stand on his perch and watch them scurry about or become completely absorbed in making a bright bauble stay where they placed it. "We have to work fast tonight," he said. "I'm catching the midnight to Washington, and I have to meet Jim at the office first."

"Why, Don, you didn't tell me!" Mrs. Hollister looked up from the wire she was hooking onto a red ball, and exclaimed, "You didn't mention it!"

"Frankly, darling, I didn't know it until three minutes ago." He came down from the ladder he had just mounted, kissed the top of her head and said expansively, "The president wants to see me."

"He *does*?"

She looked so pleased and proud that he would have corrected his misleading statement, had not Warren crawled out from the light socket and asked, "On Saturday? The day before Christmas? Come again, Dad. The President's gone on vacation."

"Well, maybe so," Don Hollister answered, pretending to look sheepish. "Or maybe it's the President's secretary, or the office cat. Or maybe it's just the president of a corporation who has to go over some papers in the morning. Anyway, I have to go. I'll be back by late afternoon."

"And if the real President *were* there," his wife told her family loyally, "he would invite your father to lunch. He did, once, you know."

"With twenty other attorneys. Fly to it, kids."

Hands grew busy. In no time at all, a green pine tree that had grown to full and beautiful maturity in an open field, kissed by the sun, washed clean by the rain, swayed by the wind in an abandoned dance, became a fairy thing. For a few days it would shimmer and shine, a delight to behold; then, its brief life ended, the trash man would cart it away. A tiny seed had taken root and matured for one short blaze of glory.

"I think you're putting too many lights at the back," Mrs. Hollister mentioned critically, as her husband balanced at a precarious angle on the ladder. "We won't have enough for the front."

"Putting plenty of lights in the back," he returned, straining to adjust a long, looping arrangement, "is the important part of trimming a tree. Depth. If you look through, you see lights.

If everything's hung on the front, what would you see back there?"

"I don't know," she admitted doubtfully. "Window curtains in the daytime, I suppose, and some tinsel at night."

"Exactly. Dick, hook another string onto the end of this one and poke some bulbs in close to the trunk, then bring it through to me. Good boy. Bobo?"

"*Yes, sir!*" Bobo had waited patiently for the decorating to come down to his level, and he lunged at the tree with such eagerness that his father dodged.

"Confound it, boy!" he yelled, as he grabbed a branch and set light bulbs chattering against each other. "You're going to ruin the whole darned business. Stand still."

"O.K., boss man."

Mrs. Hollister always thought it a miracle that the tree ever got trimmed at all, or that it looked halfway presentable when it was finished. Too many people had too many ideas, and too often disturbed someone else's special display. The tree always had a patchy look. Buff's semicircle of lower branches was artistic and studied, Bobo's a collection of anything left over. The middle looked much as a tree should look. The top? After the head of the household had affixed his star and proper lighting, the top belonged to anyone who had a long arm. Tinsel and dripping tinfoil strips blurred the bad spots and pulled the whole thing together—at least until Down Boy passed by a few times.

"I thought I heard the doorbell," she broke off her contented musing to say, listening. "Who could be dropping in this evening?"

"I'll get it." Cinda passed her string of tinsel to Bobo, who looked so grateful that she added a whole new bolt before she went on to the hall.

Paul was standing under the porch light; and as she threw open the door she tried to hide her amazement by exclaiming, "Well, hello!"

"I just stopped by on my way to the bus," he said, holding out a large, square package, "to bring you this. I can't stay."

"Oh." Cinda reached out, not knowing from his words if the box was for her or if he might be delivering it for Mr. Peterson. It was definitely candy, from the weight of it and Mr. Peterson's blue wrapping paper, and quite a lot of it, too. "Why, thank you," she said. "I mean—who's is it?"

"It's yours. Merry Christmas!"

"Oh, Paul, come *in*!"

She threw the door open as far as it would go, as if the draft would pull him inside, but he shook his head. "I can't," he answered. "I'm catching the eight-forty bus home. I only wanted to say 'Merry Christmas,' Cinda."

"Oh, Merry Christmas to you, and thank you. Paul . . . " He looked so lonely standing under the porch light, just catching a bus, with nobody to see him off and nobody to welcome him at the other end, that she asked breathlessly " . . . could you wait while I grab a coat? We're running out of icicles for the tree and I'll have to go to the dime store. It's right by the bus station, and we could walk along together."

"Why, sure. But oughtn't I bring you back?"

"Jinx will."

She set her candy on the hall table, remembered Bobo and Down Boy, and removed it to safety on top of the mantel. "We're trimming the tree," she said, diving into the closet and pulling her coat from a hanger. "I wish you could stay."

"I do, too." He could see a corner of the library from where he stood, but he looked away from it to watch Cinda wrap a scarf over her head and throw the ends back over her shoulders.

"I'll have to tell Jinx I'm going on and where I'll be," she said, leaning around the archway and calling attention to herself by shouting, "Hey, Jinx!"

Seven people stopped what they were doing and turned their heads; and Lindsey asked, "Is it for me?"

"No. I just want to tell you," she enunciated clearly and distinctly, "that I am going to the dime store for that tinfoil stuff. I will meet you there."

"Why?"

He left the tree but she ran out and slammed the door behind her. "Golly, Paul," she said as they crossed the porch, "you shouldn't have brought me such a *big* box of candy."

"I wanted it big. When I think of you," he said simply, "I think big. And I've been thinking of you a lot, lately."

"I didn't know you had," she answered, surprised, walking down the driveway and turning onto the sidewalk beside him. "I thought perhaps you were sorry we'd gone for a walk together."

"Sorry! Why should I be? Why, that was the best thing that ever happened to me." He looked down on the top of her plaid scarf bobbing along beside him, and explained, "It started me off on the right track. Up to then I'd done nothing but grouse to myself. But after I'd talked to you—and you were so darned sensible and sweet—I said to myself, 'Paul Banning, you slug, it's time you stopped pitying yourself and acting like a dim-wit.' I made up my mind that I wasn't going to cry on your shoulder, ever again. It's a fine thing when a guy's so full of his troubles that he has to cry on a girl's shoulder."

"I don't know," Cinda said soberly. "Lots of guys have done it. Men come home from wars and let their wives see the tears in their hearts. They bring their business worries home, too, and all the hundreds of little problems they have. Children cry in their mothers' arms, and the bumps don't hurt so much. Maybe, Paul," she said, looking up, "it was right for you to cry on my shoulder. And maybe it was good for me to feel hurt and sorry inside. I'm not very old, but I'm going to be a woman, someday."

She wanted so very much to make him know that his unhappiness had touched her. Her eyes looked softly up and she put her cold little hand in his as they walked along. "You're coming back to school, aren't you?" she asked. "You won't run off and join the army, will you?"

"I'm coming back." He tucked their coupled hands into his big pocket, and said with his head high, as much in promise to himself as to her, "I've got a plan worked out, and I'll make a go of it. I won't tell you what it is, yet, because I've got a fight coming up at home. I guess, Cinda," he said, grinning at her, "you're right about one thing: you're going to grow into a woman—and I'll have to grow into a man. I have to do it a little sooner than you, that's all, and standing on my own two feet."

"You can stand on a piece of mine." She stuck one shoe out, broke their stride and tripped them both. "I guess you can't," she laughed, hopping along. "It hurts too much. But if things go wrong, please feel free to cry on my shoulder."

"Boo-hoo!" he wept, dropping his face onto the soft alpaca and getting them more out of step than they were.

"Paul." She reached across with her free hand to give his cold hair a couple of sympathetic pats, then pushed his chin up to look at him. "You aren't going to fight with your father, are you?"

"You bet I am, if I have to." His head jerked upright, but he said in a calm, conversational tone, "The old man and I won't be riding the same train from here on. He'll go his way and I'll go mine. Don't ask me any questions about it—just let me say that I've been a busy boy these last few days, and I think I'm all set."

"Will I see you during the holidays?"

"Perhaps. I don't know."

"Will you come in to our party?" she persisted. "We're sure to have one, with a house full of guests. Just a rumpus, dancing affair."

"Didn't you know I'm the mambo king? If you'll let me know when . . . Oh, gosh, there goes my bus!"

They had reached the lighted intersection, and a long gray bus was pulling away from the gasoline station where it picked up passengers. He jerked Cinda's hand out of his pocket, almost flung it at her, and began to run. "Let me know," he called back. "Merry Christmas."

"Merry . . . " The bus had stopped, its doors were opening, and she didn't know where he lived. "Hey!" she shouted, as it started on again. "Wait a minute!" She ran as fast as she could, her coat flying open in the wind, watching the bus and trying to keep up with it, until she banged flat against a lamppost.

He was gone. And she hadn't thought once of the confession she had planned to make! And she couldn't invite him to her party, or even write him a nice little note to thank him for the candy. She watched the bus's taillights grow dimmer and dimmer before she unclasped the post and turned her head to find Lindsey parked by the curb.

"You look like a loose-leaf notebook in the wind," he said, remarking on her disarray. "How come you and the post got so attached to each other?"

"We met by accident." The taillights were part of many, now, and she asked, "Where does that fool bus go?"

"All the way to Reading, Pennsylvania." He cranked up the window, opened the door, and said by way of suggestion, "If you aren't planning to lean there all night, you'd be more comfortable in the car."

"I guess so." She waited while he slid over to his own side of the seat and made room for her, then plopped in and said with a sigh, "Paul Banning's on it. You don't know where he lives, do you?"

"Nope. Haven't you ever had sense enough to ask him?"

"I haven't had time. He keeps popping in and out of my life—now you see him, now you don't—and he always takes off so suddenly. I can't even thank him for my candy."

"Is *that* where the box of delicious chocolates came from?" Lindsey asked, smacking his lips as he started his motor. "We sure have enjoyed it!"

"You haven't!" Cinda sat up and cried. "You didn't *open* it!"

"Why not? Bobo brought it in, and Mom said, 'Oh, how thoughtful of Mr. Peterson to remember us on Christmas,' and we all had some. I think Down Boy finished the top layer."

"I can't bear it." Cinda looked about to cry. "It was the biggest box of candy I ever had," she mourned, "and the first one from a boy. I was going to pass it around, then make it last a long, long time."

Her poor little face looked so pitiful, with her scarf pushed back and her hair standing on end, that Lindsey relented. "It's right on the mantel where you left it," he assured her. "Nothing's happened to it, and Down Boy hasn't come home, yet." And when she leaned back with a thankful sigh, he added, "Cousin Maud phoned right after you left. They aren't coming for Christmas."

Cinda didn't know whether she felt relief or disappointment. Paula, as another girl, was fun; but shut up in a house with three boys, she might set off an explosion that would put a carload of firecrackers to shame—notwithstanding the careful warning to

Dick. The male sex, Cinda had discovered, was practically immune to warnings. So she asked, "Are you sorry?"

"Pleased. Cousin Maud gets on my nerves. Yak, yak, yak. I'm sorry the old girl got the virus, but I'm glad she has it in her own bed. Paula, by the way, is spending Christmas with her family and flying in on the twenty-seventh."

"She is? All by herself?" Cinda rolled her eyes around at Lindsey. He was hunched over the wheel, watching ahead, but she thought his heavy shoulders and broad face looked set. "I wonder if she'll like Dick," she murmured, testing.

"Oh, sure." He swung the car into the driveway, stopped at the steps, then remembered his berth beside the garage, and lurched into gear again. "He'll have mints of money to spend on her," he growled.

"What makes you think so?"

"His Christmas packages I carried in. One little box was mailed from Tiffany's, and a big one from Brooks Brothers. Brooks Brothers, no less! Where Dad gets his clothes. If by any chance I should get a new tux," he said sadly, "mine'll come from Macy's."

"Oh, no it won't!" Cinda cried, trying to be too helpful, as usual. "Moth showed it to me and . . . "

She stopped too late, but it seemed he hadn't heard her. "Mom," he said, "pipes up like the perfect little hostess, 'Consider us your family, Dick,' and he certainly does. He skittered out to get her another cup of coffee before she even knew she wanted it, and presented it to her like a waiter at the Waldorf. Sugar and cream, and even a paper napkin. And he always happens to be right beside the ladder when Dad's about to fall off. When Paula gets a load of him, she's going down for the count."

"Oh, no, she isn't, Jinx." This, thought Cinda, is a disguised but excellent example of crying on a girl's shoulder. She felt pleased to have Lindsey bowed so low, but, rising to the apt quotation that "Woman's work is never done," she consoled reliably, "I have a hunch that Dick won't waste much time on Paula, because he'll think Melody Ayer is the most attractive girl in town."

"He'll never get a chance to meet her."

"Oh, but he will. My hunch says that he'll leave Paula strictly alone."

"Did you tell him to?"

"Not exactly. I only said . . . "

"You dumb dodo!" He jerked on the brake and hit the wheel so hard with his elbow that the horn brayed into the night. "Why can't you ever learn to keep out of my affairs!" he yelled, flinging the door open and himself onto the gravel.

"Well, my goodness, Jinx, wait a minute." Cinda hopped out, too, and ran around the back of the car, asking as she went, "Now, how would Dick ever know that you're the only one who's crazy about Paula? War-Horse lives here, too."

"Did you tell him I am?"

"Well, I simply said . . . "

He started for the house and she ran along beside him, coaxing, "Please listen. I brought up Melody's name because I thought it would give him someone to look forward to meeting. Melody was the main topic of conversation," she panted, offering her own private life as a sacrifice. "I thought if he could take her away from Page it would help me. Oh, Jinx," she implored, trying to remember exactly what she *had* said, "I don't think I mentioned much about you and—and War-Horse."

He still stalked toward the back porch in wounded silence, so she ducked under a clothesline and tagged along. So help me, she promised herself, when he flung the kitchen door open and she scooted in behind him, I'll never say anything to anybody, ever again. I never will. I'll make it a New Year's resolution. Paula can go off and elope with Dick or War-Horse, and I won't stop them. I won't care if Jinx has a nervous breakdown. I'm through.

Lindsey had turned into the library and closed the door behind him, so she went on to the front hall. Her box of candy was where she had left it; and, taking it down, she decided that the quickest way to win back Lindsey's affection was by making a gay entrance and passing it around. He liked candy, but that couldn't be helped. He liked it too well, she thought ruefully, as she tore off the wrapper and carefully worked the beautiful red ribbon and bow loose without untying it.

Holding the box in front of her, as if it were a peace offering made of her own bleeding heart, she sailed into the library and went to Lindsey first of all.

Chapter VI

The magic hour of Christmas morning was over. Weeks of pushing through crowded stores with other shoppers, of hunting just exactly the right gifts, then wrapping them artistically and tying them with yards and yards of bright ribbon, had ended in a litter of paper on the floor.

Each Hollister sat beside his or her personal acquisitions, and Mr. Hollister took one last look behind the tree for a stray package, then said, "That's it. We've had it."

"It was a fine Christmas," his elderly, gray-haired father remarked, as he did every year, sitting on the divan beside his wife and patting her plump knee. "Did you get everything you wanted, Cynthia?"

"More than I wanted," she answered, nodding her carefully waved, blue-white head.

"Seems as if your pile's kind of small," he said ruefully, "compared to mine."

"That's because cultured pearls and perfume take up much less room between us than a hunting coat."

She looked like a pleasant little pouter pigeon, sitting with her small feet not quite touching the floor; and she asked, "Do you like the coat?"

"Man, it's cool," he praised, copying the remark Lindsey had made when his new tuxedo had come out of its box. "Nobody's going to mistake me for a deer in this bright red."

He stood up to slip the coat on over his tweed jacket, a big man, straight and tall in his late sixties; and Warren stopped taking practice swings with a new golf club to help him into it. "They'll think you're a forest fire, Gramps," he said.

"Or a Canadian Mountie. Let's see what the rest of you got."

Everyone began arranging displays like salesmen setting out their samples. The old gentleman paused beside Cinda first, letting his eyes feast on a pink confection, billowing out of its open box. "Mighty pretty," he said, casting about for one of the finer points of a dress to mention. "I like that ruffled thing around the neck."

"It isn't around the neck," Cinda laughed, hopping up from the floor to hold the pink gown in front of her. "See? This is a dropped shoulder, and these are tiny, tiny net ruchings."

"They look like cotton candy. What else have you?"

"Oh, sweaters, stationery, perfume, the lapel watch I've already thanked you and Gram for, and simply adore. And Gramps," she stood on tiptoe to kiss him on the cheek, and say, "Thanks for the usual check."

"Pshaw, I guess you did all right." He turned to Bobo who sat cross-legged on the floor, his autoharp still across his lap. "Well, well, boy," he said, "that's quite a zither."

"It's not a zither, Gramps," Bobo corrected, lost in the wonderment of so many strings to strum and buttons to push. "It's an autoharp, and we're using them in school, now. They're *something*!"

"I reckon you'll be playing in the orchestra in no time at all," his grandfather said, noticing the other gifts Bobo had had no time to admire as yet, his check among them. "Well, Warren, are you going to take my picture?"

"Sure, Gramps." Warren laid down his golf club and unslung

his camera case from around his shoulder. "I thought I would, just as soon as everybody settles down a little," he said, meaning especially his mother and father, who were trying to assemble a portable nest of tables designed for television dining.

"The thing's no good," Donald Hollister complained loudly, wishing he had his money back. "Look at it!"

"It works this way, sir." Dick finished strapping on his new watch and stepped over the box from Brooks Brothers, which held only a new wool dressing gown and not the expensive dinner jacket Lindsey had been sure would come out of it. "My mother has a set of these, and the tables fit in upside down, like this."

He reversed the tables, rehung the trays, and said, "There you are," as Gramps followed along to ask,

"How was your Christmas, boy?"

"Fine, sir." Dick showed his watch and pointed to the neckties and yellow sleeveless sweater Mrs. Hollister had rushed out and bought. "I had a big Christmas," he said. "And my folks phoned me yesterday. Yesterday was Christmas over where they are, you know."

"Why, so it was."

"And they're going to call again on New Year's day—on our New Year's day, this time. I'd like to thank you again for the cuff links that you and Mrs. Hollister gave me."

"And I'd like to thank you again for the pipe tobacco." Mr. Hollister gave Dick's shoulder a pat, and looked down at Buff who was standing close beside him. "My, my, my, what a beautiful child," he said, beaming on the doll she held up to him. "What's her name?"

"I think it's Carol," Buff answered thoughtfully. "She was born on Christmas, you know. I used to have a little girl named

Carol, but she—she had an accident. Will you hold her, Gramps, while I take one of the big cartons around and pile the paper into it? It's my job."

He took the doll gingerly, surprised to find its body as soft and pliable as a live baby's. "What do they make 'em of, nowadays?" he inquired. "Human flesh?"

Buff laughed and started to take off her new red coat, then darted across the room and pulled loose an envelope from the handlebars of a new bicycle. "Bend down a minute, Gramps," she said when she ran back. "I want to tell you something."

She pulled his head close to her lips, and, with her arms around his neck, whispered, "I love you, Gramps. Not because of the bicycle and the check. I just do. I'm going to keep the check forever, in memory of you."

"You'd better deposit it in a bank." Young as he felt, he couldn't stay bent over too long, not holding a doll and with Buff pulling on him, so he said, "I want you to enjoy the ten dollars, little girl. That's what it's for. Let's see what Lindsey got."

"All right."

Buff put the check in her coat pocket, and, like a trash man turned loose in a sea of prosperity, began dragging her carton. Mr. Hollister went on to look at the four new tires and seat covers Lindsey had for his car, then laid the doll on his wife's lap. "Here, great-grammaw," he said. "You hold the baby a while." Then he turned to put an arm fondly around his daughter-in-law. "Was Santa Claus good to you, Frances?" he asked.

"He's always too good, Dad."

She put her arm around him, too, patting the bulky red coat, as she said, "Having you and Mother with us makes it Christmas."

The Hollisters had been her parents for more years than she had been married. Her own father had been killed in the First World War, and just before she had come East to college, her mother had died. Fate has a strange way of deciding which two people are meant for each other, then seeing that they meet. It had had to try three times before it got Frances Warren to Princeton and a dance. And even then it had been forced to rush a very nice young man to the hospital with appendicitis, so it could shove Donald Hollister in as a substitute. Three weeks later they were so sure that no one else in the whole world would do for either of them, that Donald drove her to Glenvale and announced, "Mother, Dad, you've always wanted a daughter, so I'm getting you the best one I can find."

It was a whole year before Frances Warren became Mrs. Donald J. Hollister, but she had two loving parents during that time.

"You and Mother really spoiled the children this year," she said, thinking of the watch, the bicycle, the tires, the camera, and the expensive telescope that Bobo would discover when the novelty of the autoharp wore off. "I was so eager to watch Stella open the box with the fur stole in it," she went on, "that I almost asked her not to spend the night at her sister's. And thank you, darlings, for my pearls. I think," she said, fingering the strand, "that they're even prettier than yours, Mother, and I helped Dad choose yours."

She looked down at Buff, moving along on all fours and trying to reach a piece of paper under the divan, and cried, "Mercy, child, don't throw away the *ribbon!* You know Stella saves it."

"I'm only getting rid of the paper kind. The rest is in this box I carry around with me," Buff explained. "See?"

As she lifted a brown cardboard lid, Bobo let out a yell.

"That's mine!" he howled, scrambling across the rug. "My harp came in that box! You give it back."

"All right. *There*!" Buff dumped the neatly folded pieces of ribbon on the floor and threw the box at him. "You can pick up the rest of the trash, you horrid, selfish, boy!" she cried.

"Aw, shut up."

Bobo inspected his precious box for damages, found none, and had started to crawl back to his own corner when his mother said gently, "Children. Not on Christmas."

"O.K., I'm sorry," he wrenched out reluctantly. "I guess she didn't do it on purpose. O.K., Buff?"

"You hurt my feelings." Buff took her doll from her grandmother, nestled her cheek into curls that were guaranteed against soap and water and anything a child could do to them, and sighed, "I guess I'd better not try to help any more."

"We'll all help."

Frances Hollister reached down for crumpled pieces of paper near her; Cinda brought another box for the ribbon; and after Bobo had laid his harp to safe rest in its rightful bed, he carried out the carton.

Warren took flashlight pictures. Everyone stood around the tree for one; those who were able, sat on the floor for another. They sang carols at the piano, they pretended to be teaching Buff to ride a bicycle. And halfway through the film, something went wrong inside the camera's complicated mechanism.

"Gosh darn," Warren said, twisting uselessly and not moving the film an inch. "The paper's caught. I'll have to take it in the coat closet and open the back."

"You haven't time," his father informed him, glad the whole affair had been brought to a sudden end. "Church in thirty minutes. Is everyone ready?"

No one was. Some sped upstairs, some contented themselves

with hasty grooming in the lavatory beside the basement stairs; and everyone chose a table or the piano as safe spots to deposit valuable loot. Anything made of cloth, wood, paper, or stainless steel was delectable to Down Boy, who had set up a dismal howling in the kitchen and would push open the pantry door as soon as he discovered he could chew his rope in two.

Church was sweet and solemn, the quiet hush spiced with the tang of evergreens. Candles, along the altar and below the great stained glass window, shone their steady light upward on the benevolent figure of the loving Christ, carrying a small, lost lamb in his arms. Hollisters, in a long line that filled a pew, bowed their heads for a moment in silent prayer, then found their hymnals and sang joyously of God's love for His children.

"Mother." Buff tugged at her mother's coat sleeve as ushers carried silver plates up the aisles. During the long sermon her eyes had never left the window above the rector's head; and she whispered, "This is Jesus's birthday. I want to give him a present."

"Yes, darling." Mrs. Hollister was opening her purse, and she said, "In just a minute, dear."

"But I mean a present from *me*," Buff whispered again. "I have such a lot of presents, Mother, and I haven't thought of God or Jesus once, not even when we were singing the carols at home. I just thought about my doll and how pretty I looked, singing. Mother, I want to give Him this."

She took the envelope from her pocket and carefully extracted the check her grandfather had written for her. "You can't, darling," her mother leaned over to explain. "It's made out to you, not the church. I'll give you a dollar for the offering."

"But I have to do good, kind things," Buff protested. "God told me so. Jesus helped people. I haven't helped anybody."

Tears gathered in her eyes, and she sat clutching the check

while Cinda, on her other side, leaned down, too. "Yes, you have, Buff," Cinda comforted. "You helped pack the baskets Moth sent to Mrs. Toomy and the Selfridges. And you were happy when Daddy took care of the janitor's hospital bill and Moth sent fifty dollars out to the orphanage."

"But it wasn't anything from *me*. I didn't care, really." The tears were rolling faster, now, and Buff's little hands clamped the piece of paper so hard they trembled. She swallowed a sob, and tears dripped onto her new red coat as she looked up at the little lamb cradled so tenderly in the Good Shepherd's arms.

A silver plate had almost reached them when Mrs. Hollister leaned out and looked along her pew. "Did any of you bring a pen?" she whispered.

Six hands holding folded bills paused in mid-air, then Buff's father took the plate, laid his offering and fountain pen on top, and passed it on to her. "Sign your name on the back, Buff, dear," Mrs. Hollister said, laying the check on her hymnal and watching Buff make round childish letters. "Cinda, give the plate to the usher on your aisle."

Cinda knew people were craning forward to see what was causing such a delay in the Hollister pew, but she took time to return her dollar bill to her purse and extract the five dollars she had been saving for her class ring. Then she passed one of her new Christmas handkerchiefs to Buff and watched her dab away her tears. Buff was truly a strange child, she thought once again. And it occurred to her that God had had a very good reason for putting Buff where He had, and that He must love her very dearly.

"Here, honey," she said, opening her hymnal and standing up to share it.

The organ swelled out its glad music, and another hour in a glorious day had passed. Church was over.

Dinner, thanks to Stella's having cooked the turkey ahead of time, and to a freezer and a modern stove that timed its own cooking while people went off to church, was bustling confusion for a while. But even dinner ended as the Christmas tree had, in repletion. It left soiled plates instead of torn paper, and had an electric dishwasher to dispose of them instead of a cardboard carton.

By three o'clock the Hollister house was almost empty. Cinda was the only one left; and she was in the downstairs hall, putting on her best brown coat and the mite of a hat she had worn to church, when the doorbell rang.

"I'm sorry, but my father isn't here," she said, looking at the registered, special delivery letter a postman held out to her. "He and my mother are over at the Bromfields'. Can you take it there?"

The postman looked cold and tired. It was a dreary way to spend your Christmas, she thought. And she said hastily, "Just give it to me, I'll sign for it and take it."

"Why, thanks. Merry Christmas."

"Merry Christmas, to you."

The letter changed hands, she scrawled an illegible name in his book, and was watching him tramp over the soggy dead grass to his car at the curb, when another car turned into the driveway. This one was painted a bright canary yellow.

Oh, gracious me, Jinx isn't home, was her first panicked reaction. He won't want to stay without Jinx. She almost closed the door, then jerked it open and stood watching Page come up the steps. "Where's Melody?" was the only greeting that came into her head.

"How do I know? Is Jinx here?"

"Hunh-uh." She blinked a little, dazzled by such close proximity to someone in a brown leather coat and cap, then recovered enough to say, "No one is. I'm the only one—and I'm taking a letter to Dad at the Bromfields'."

"I'll drive you over."

He turned back as if he expected her to join him; but never having had such an invitation before, she stood rooted to the spot. "Oh, I can walk," she said. "And anyway, I'm going on to Kitty Lou's. Thanks, just the same."

"Come on, I haven't anything to do."

Here was her chance to ride in one of the bucket seats, right down on the leather, instead of held in by Jinx! Straight through the middle of town, in the daylight. "Oh, thanks," she breathed; and caught her coat in the door in her hurry to close it.

Never had she been handed into anything so fine. In fact, she never had been handed into any car before, or had the folds of her coat arranged around her, the window cranked up.

"Hope you won't be cold with the top down," Page said, opening the low door on his side and sliding under the wheel.

"Oh, it's fine." She slid down as far as she could, feeling like a turtle peeking out of its shell, and thinking how gay her hat would look to pedestrians as it flashed along, a bright red dot on top of a brown mound.

"You may get a little wind," he said, starting off with such a roar that the red dot almost blew off before anyone had a chance to see it.

Cinda thought his warning a masterpiece of understatement. Her mouth had been open in a smile, and the cold air that went in and down into her lungs took her breath away. She could only squint her eyes and nod, then clamp a bare hand over her hat.

It was better when they turned onto the Bromfields' short street because the wind was behind them. Quite a lot of it managed to circle around and blow over the windshield, but she was able to shout, "Did you have a nice Christmas?"

"So-so. Which house is it?"

"The brick one, on the next corner."

The car slowed to a pleasant pace, and stopped. "Well, thank you," she said, waiting just long enough to see if she would get the princess treatment again, and finding she wouldn't. "Jinx should be home around four."

"Hustle in and I'll wait. I haven't anything to do. Have you?" he asked as an afterthought.

"Not until the gang starts coming. Well . . . I'll hurry."

She wondered what under the sun had become of Melody. To sit in that car was like taking the President's seat when he got up for a drink of water; and as she handed her father's letter to Mr. Bromfield, she half-expected that Melody would pop up somewhere along the route to Kitty Lou's and pull her out. But it didn't happen.

"How about a ride around Country Club Drive?" Page asked, when she had got herself in and settled again, her thin, church-going gloves on, this time. "We go right past Kitty Lou's if you want to stop there."

"Oh, no, it doesn't matter." Kitty Lou's Christmas present was at home on the hall table, so she said, "She's coming over later, anyway;" and the car roared on again.

It hadn't picked up full speed when it passed the Chappells' white clapboard house; and although Cinda knew it for an almost impossible wish, she nevertheless wished that Kitty Lou might just happen to be standing idly at a front window, her eyes trained on the street.

Of course she wasn't. The white house flashed by and straight streets became winding roads, and, too quickly, open country.

There was even more wind in the country. The bright glow of riding beside Page had long ago faded into cold shivers that raced each other up and down Cinda's spine under the thin silk of her dress. She slid even lower in the seat, turned up the collar of her coat, and managed to pull out her scarf and tie up her head and hat in white silk.

Page seemed bent on making a record run to the Glenvale Country Club. He swung into its semicircular driveway, scanning the parked cars as he passed them; and when Cinda, in a sudden burst of understanding, silently pointed to the Ayers' blue and gray sedan, he swung out again.

It's no wonder Melody stays in where it's warm, she thought miserably, as they breezed toward town again, shooting a watery glance at Page in his warm leather coat, heavy shoes, long pants, and a helmet. It's not worth it. If my teeth ever stop chattering, I'll tell him I want to go home.

She clamped them together and managed to point again when they came to her street, thankful that Page obediently slowed the car. And when he pulled up beside the dear, beautiful, Hollister steps, she rammed stiff fingers into her pocket and felt for her handkerchief. Buff had kept it after church, so she wiped her eyes on her scarf and climbed out on two numb stumps of feet.

"Th-th-thank you," she chattered, wondering why she bothered. After all, cars did have tops to put up for girls in thin clothes, and they had heaters. And they didn't have to go streaking along like a jet, either, just because Page Vandergren had had a quarrel with Melody Ayer. It made her mad!

Never, in all her wildest imaginings, had she thought she would have the opportunity to be angry with Page—much less, to tell him so. "I hope," she said, with her face stiff, "I'm never enough of an idiot to go riding with you again."

"Gee, Cinda, I'm sorry. I didn't think about your being cold."

She gave him a long, searching look of appraisal. "I guess you didn't," she agreed. Then she saw Warren and Dick coming from the garage.

Warren clapped Page on the shoulder, Dick admired the sleek car and watched Cinda clumping toward the steps. "What happened to you?" he asked.

"I'm frozen stiff," she answered, glad her face had some feeling in it again. "Like a dope, I went on a Christmas Day outing."

"To the rescue, men!" Dick took one arm, Warren the other, and together they swung her up the steps. "There you are," Dick said, when they let her down at the door.

She didn't care if Page came in or went off to hunt Melody again, but she felt it only decent to try and grin at him, and he came bounding up the steps.

"Cinda," he said, when they were in the hall and she was seated on the radiator, "I'm sorry, I truly am. I was mad at Melody, and I didn't give a darn if you got cold, or not."

"Oh, that's all right." Her body felt warmer and was tingling nicely. "Why don't you go get her and make up?" she suggested.

"I don't want to. I'd rather be with you."

"Oh." She took a cup of hot tea from Dick and winked up at him. "This is your chance to move in," she said. "I can arrange a date for you."

She had expected her offer to send Page leaping off into action, but, to her sorrow, it didn't. He simply sat down on the radiator, too, and took a sip of her tea.

Only a few last rays of late sunlight played on the landing windows, for Christmas afternoon was almost ended. An evening of fun and dancing lay ahead. And, drinking her tea, Cinda slowly began to thaw out and look forward to it.

Chapter VII

"I THINK it was mean of you to go ridin' with Page and not tell me," Kitty Lou pouted, the morning after Christmas, sitting on one of Cinda's beds and watching her put on a new green skirt and yellow twin sweaters.

"Goodness knows, I wish you'd had my seat." Cinda debated between a flat, gold necklace and a pearl choker, as Kitty Lou went on:

"And the way you kept him attached to you all evenin'. I never thought you would be so selfish!"

"I didn't keep him attached." She chose the pearls; and said, clasping them under the lace-trimmed collar of her blouse, "You know just as well as I do that he had had a row with Melody and was showing her how little he cared. I couldn't help it if . . . "

"If he followed you around like a pet poodle? All the way to the first floor, all the way back up again. Down for the tray of sandwiches, up with the extra cokes, up with the kettle of hot chocolate, down with the paper cups and plates. Weren't Jinx, or War-Horse, or Dick, supposed to do *anything*?"

"They were busy. Dick was keeping Melody happy, and War-Horse had his own gang in and couldn't be bothered with us. I thought Jinx," she said proudly, "was a darned good host—the way he ran the record player and was always ready to play table tennis, or do anything anybody suggested. Excuse me."

She leaned across Kitty Lou for her purse, and said as she came up, "I'll have to leave you, now, but if you want to stick around, I can promise you that the great Page Vandergren will be here at eleven o'clock. He's going to watch Jinx put the new tires on his car. You can watch, too."

"Where are you goin'?"

Kitty Lou still sat on the bed as Cinda went back to her dressing table. "I," Cinda said, running a comb through her hair again and checking her lipstick, to be sure she had on enough, but not enough to be too noticeable, "have an errand to do."

"Where?" It suddenly penetrated Kitty Lou's consciousness that Cinda's toilet on a holiday morning had been extensive and too careful. "I'll bet you're pullin' a fast one an' are goin' to meet Page," she accused.

"My pet, I'm going to see an old lady." Cinda considered her good coat against her alpaca, and opened her closet door. "I am calling on Paul's grandmother," she said, taking her brown coat from its hanger. "To ask his address, so I can invite him to our big bust tomorrow night."

"Why don't you call her up?"

"Because . . . " Cinda hated to admit that she was curious about the inside of the Banning house, that she wanted to see the drawing room and hoped to be invited to view the ballroom with its crystal chandeliers and gold chairs. Even more, she hated to say that she planned to have a word or two with Paul's grandmother, to tell the old lady how much the younger generation liked her grandson, and how very much he needed to mingle with it. "Moth said I could take the car," she hedged zestfully. "It's still exciting to drive myself somewhere."

"Want me to go along?"

"No, this is your chance to snag Page. It will prove to you," she pointed out, as they went down the stairway, "that I didn't mean to be selfish. You stick around, and I'll bet he'll drive you home."

"All right." Kitty Lou accepted so promptly that Cinda felt almost mean at the ease with which she had got rid of her.

"Look," she said, when they reached the bottom landing and the big, colored glass window, "you choose a stone and make a wish. I've done it all my life, and it works fine. I'll make one, too."

"Will you make it for me?"

"I can't." Cinda shook her head. "I have to make it for someone else, this morning," she said, choosing a sparkling sapphire and closing her eyes as she rubbed her finger over it. "There. Don't take that ruby nearest you. I used it yesterday, and Stella *did* come home and show us her Christmas presents without crying, even the fur stole. Try that topaz up above you. It's had a good rest."

Kitty Lou reached up and rubbed the topaz, looking so wistful that Cinda hoped Page wouldn't forget his promise to bring over his fancy car jack. "Well, rest yourself and have a nice time," she said. "I'll be back as soon as I can."

"Don't hurry."

There was a large chair by a front window; and Kitty Lou was headed for it, planning to sit under a holly wreath until nightfall if need be. So Cinda let herself out and began a careful drive along Elmwood Avenue.

She hugged the curb, hovered so long at intersections that hurrying motorists behind her blew their horns in exasperation, and, not trusting her direction lights, she waved her hand out the window when she had to make a turn. And when she reached two wrought iron gateposts near the end of Cedar Lane, she swung her wheel and aimed straight between them. It was a relief to put on her brake under a high but almost-too-narrow-for-the-modern-car *porte-cochere.*

But she was destined not to see the ballroom, or more than a patch of drawing room at the end of a long corridor. She had come to the wrong door, it seemed. This was a side door, far away from the main part of the house. Guests, in good weather, were supposed to sweep along a branch of the driveway and enter across a tiled terrace in front.

An old man opened the door before she could ring the bell. He wore a green felt apron, such as she had seen foreign servants wear in movies, and he asked, "Yes?"

"I'd like to see Mrs. Banning, please."

"*Madame* is not at home."

He blocked the opening in the door, but through the glass panel Cinda could see a stately figure, warmly wrapped in a knitted lavender shawl, step down from the last and only visible step of a stairway, and come toward her.

"I won't keep her but a minute," she said, recognizing that Indian walk. "I only want to ask about her grandson."

"Very good."

He held the door open, and as she stepped inside, Mrs. Banning called, "What is it, André?"

"It's me, Mrs. Banning," Cinda answered, taking a few steps forward and introducing herself. "I'm Cinda Hollister. Donald and Frances Hollister's daughter, over on Elmwood Avenue. I think you know my grandparents, too."

"Ah, yes."

Mrs. Banning stopped and waited inquiringly. She stood wrapped in her shawl, making no move to invite Cinda along the passage, and a deep but querulous voice whined from somewhere, "Who is it, Sally?"

"Someone to see Paul, I imagine dear. I shan't be but a minute."

"I–I wanted to ask Paul's phone number," Cinda said, wishing she had followed Kitty Lou's advice and conducted her inquiry by telephone. "We're having a party tomorrow night and we want him to come, but I don't know where he lives."

"He hasn't told you?"

"No, you see–well, the bus left so fast, and school's closed, so I can't look it up there, and my mother said, 'Dear me, it's been ten years since I was on the garden club committee with his mother.' She can't remember. So Jinx and I thought–Lindsey, I mean . . ." Cinda gave up trying to make a halting explanation into such an inscrutable stare, and ended, "I thought I'd ask you."

"Do you know my grandson?"

"Oh, yes. We like him very much." Here was her chance to grab a bear by the tail; and Cinda was ready. But before she could give more than a good yank by saying, "We want him to know our gang and have some fun," the bear, as bears usually will, turned and bit her.

"I feel you should leave that to Paul," Mrs. Banning said crisply. "I'm sure he would have given you his address, had he wanted you to have it. It is very kind of you to wish to invite him to your party, and I shall pass the invitation on when I talk with his mother. If he cares to come I am sure he will get in touch with you."

"But . . ." Cinda felt a cold draft on her back and knew André had opened the door again. "Mrs. Banning," she found courage to say, "Paul's not a little boy. He's a very good friend of mine. And it's my fault that I don't know where he lives in the country. I knew where he lived in town. I asked him to my party and he wants to come, so I think I should have the chance to tell him when it's to be. I'm sorry—but I do."

The querulous voice whined again in the distance, and Mrs. Banning said, "André, see what Mr. Banning wants. I'll let Miss—Miss . . ."

"Cinda Hollister."

"I'll let Miss Hollister out."

André took a step, but the whine grew louder, as if it might be leaving whatever room it was in and setting out along the corridor, and Mrs. Banning hurried off to stop it. "*Good* morning, Miss Hollister," she called back as she strode away. "*André, attendez.*"

As the old servant watched her go, his lined face cracked into an unaccustomed smile. It was the only smile Cinda had seen, and probably the only one the house had seen in years.

"*Ma'amselle,*" he said softly, "If you will call *Monsieur* Paul in Cranmore, you will reach him. Cranmore, one-three-nine."

"Oh, thank you."

"I should like him to come to your party. Good morning, *Ma'amselle.*"

"Good-by, André."

Cinda smiled, too, and sent him a wave as she ran down the few steps to her car. "I hope the poor old goat won't get into trouble for that," she muttered, concentrating on the job of backing out without hitting a cement pillar, turning around in the Y of a driveway, and moving out into the flow of traffic.

Mercy on us, what a place, she thought, waiting for a car to pass, then waving a signal at no one at all, and hustling onto the vacant roadway. No wonder Paul's tied up in knots. I'd go crazy.

Lindsey was standing on the side steps when she crawled her careful way along her own driveway and came to a silent stop beside him. "Paula's coming in on the two-ten," he said, opening the door and hauling her out. "We have to use this car to go to the Newark Airport to meet her."

"Where's yours?"

No gray sedan was parked in front of the garage, no tires littered the grass, no yellow convertible crouched anywhere.

"Oh, I took the tires and seat covers down to the garage," Lindsey tossed off grandly. "I'm a man of means, with the check Gramps gave me. Hurry up and grab a sandwich so we can start."

"But where's Kitty Lou? Where's Page?"

"Don't know. I called Page and told him what I'd decided to do, so he didn't come over. Mom said Kitty Cat was around for a while, but I didn't see her. Are you coming in, or not?"

"Oh, gosh." Cinda plodded up the steps, wondering what she could say to the girl who used to be her best friend. "You don't need to look so excited and happy," she groaned, "when I'm in such terrible trouble—and all because of you."

"*Me?*" He asked. "Now what have I done, this time?"

"You weren't where you said you'd be, with Page. Oh, Jinx," she sighed, "you'll simply have to wait while I make two telephone calls. Kitty Lou will never forgive me, and I want to ask Paul to our party."

"Not a chance. Paula's the name, not Paul. Planes don't wait on telephone calls."

He escorted her out to the kitchen, handed her a sandwich and pulled her coat back on when she tried to take it off. "Of course I'd rather go alone," he informed her, while she choked on a swallow of milk, "but Mom said you wanted to go."

"Why *don't* you go alone?" She put her glass down and grinned at him under a white mustache. "Go on, Jinx," she urged. "You'd like to."

But he shook his head. "Nope," he said. "Paula might think it was funny. She might think I'm trying to move in, or something. You're her friend."

"O.K., but I don't seem to be anybody's friend, right now."

Cinda knew how timid Lindsey felt. To arrive alone to meet Paula would be the same as pinning a big red heart on his chest. Warren could do it and say crossly, "Hi, there. I *would* be the one who had to drive all this way and get you;" but not Lindsey. He would be tongue-tied from being so glad.

"I'll go," she said.

As they rode along, she told him of the strange people Paul lived with. She had to tell someone. And she chattered about her miserable ride with Page, and Christmas, and Stella, and Down Boy. She chattered as if she never would stop, while Lindsey drove with one eye on the dashboard clock.

The plane was in when they parked the car and tore through the terminal building, and Paula was standing beside a porter with her bags. She looked beautiful, in her soft fur coat, hatless, her short black hair brushed back high on her forehead and fitting her head like a smooth satin cap. Her deep blue eyes with their fringe of dark lashes searched the large lobby, not concerned or anxious, but only interested in the people who passed by. She looked older than seventeen, cool, self-assured. And when Cinda cried, "Paula!" and gave her an enthusiastic hug, she returned it gently and held out a slim, gloved hand to Lindsey.

"Hello, Lindsey," she said, having refused, two summers before, ever to call him Jinx again. "I hoped you'd come, too."

"You did?" Lindsey made magnificent gestures toward the porter, the bags, and his car outside. "Just try to keep me away," he said, forgetting to let go of her hand. "War-horse went out to play golf in this sloppy mess, but not Ji—not Lindsey. Too bad I had to bring the kid along."

Everything was fine! She still liked him!

"Why don't you sit in the back?" he growled, braver now, when Cinda pushed in beside Paula, in front. "It's crowded up here."

"Because I have to tell Paula all about Dick," Cinda retorted happily, sliding down and linking her arm through Paula's. "And the party. She has to know *all about everything!*"

She and Paula talked most of the way home while he nodded now and then, and drove. It didn't matter too much. Every few minutes Paula smiled at him; and once she asked, "Who's taking me to the Country Club dance?" She even leaned a little forward to look directly at him and ask, "Are you?"

Chapter VIII

"ZIPPIDY-DOODAH, ZIPPIDY-AY," Lindsey sang lustily, leaping up the stairs and stopping to poke his head around the door of his mother's room, grinning at Cinda who sat upright on her mother's *chaise longue*, the telephone at her ear. "Meowww," he yowled softly. "Is little Kitty Cat clawing you?"

"Sh." She put her hand over the mouthpiece and said, "I'm not calling Kitty Lou. This is the other one, so go away."

It was after five-thirty, and the first chance she had had to telephone Paul. The operator had repeated her number after her, then apparently gone off for a coffee break, because nothing happened. No ringing. Just silence. She watched Lindsey charge on up to the third floor, then jiggled the little black bar until a bored voice said, "I am ringing your number: Cranmore, one, th-r-ree, ni-een." That time there was a distinct burrring noise, and Paul's voice said, "Hello?"

"Oh, *hello!*" she cried. "This is Cinda. Did you have a nice Christmas?"

"Fine," he answered. "Did you?"

"*Wonderful!* Paul, listen." She began telling him about the party, leaning back comfortably, now, and finally said, "Paula's here, and she's just darling. She's dying to meet you because your names are almost alike, you know, and Jinx says you can have the top bunk in his room tomorrow night, so plan to stay over. And we're invited out to Marty O'Conner's tomorrow for lunch and skating. Not War-Horse and Dick," she clarified with scarcely a pause for breath, "just Paula and Jinx, and you and I." She stopped and asked, "You'll come, won't you?"

"Gee, Cinda, I'd like to, but . . ."

"Then, of course, you will. Paul?"

"Yes?"

He sat on a straight French chair in the center hall and listened to her exclaim excitedly, "We've found out that you only live about twenty-five miles away and that we can pick you up, then circle back to Marty's. Could you be ready by ten o'clock?"

"I don't know," he answered carefully, knowing his mother was lying on the sofa in the living room, hearing everything he said. "You see, Dad's away and won't be home until around noon tomorrow."

"Oh, Paul."

She sounded so disappointed that he temporized, "If I could get the stock fed . . ."

"You'll just have to. You'll either have to get up in the middle of the night or not go to bed. We'll be there at ten."

"I'd rather come in on the bus. I'd rather, Cinda," he repeated. "Please, I'd rather."

"Ten o'clock, chum." Her laugh was so gay and filled with such happy satisfaction that he could only sit and listen helplessly to it. And when it was cut off with a click, he sat rubbing the telephone back and forth along his knee.

I could meet them down by the gate, he thought in despair. I could have my suitcase with me and say I wanted to save time by meeting them there. They wouldn't have to come up here. He stared unseeingly at the wall, then remembered the telephone and put it down.

"Paul?"

"Yes, Mother."

"Who called, dear?"

"A friend of mine. I'll be there in a minute."

He walked through the big, dim dining room to the kitchen and stood before the sink. It looked dark and bleak outdoors, as dark and bleak as he felt. Lonely. "I'm going tomorrow," he said, taking a glass and running cold water into it. "I'm going to Glenvale, and I'm never coming back. I can't believe it. I'll never live here again. This will never be my home."

He poured the water out without drinking it, and went slowly back to the living room.

"That was a girl, Mother," he said, turning on a lamp and sitting down on a faded damask chair before a little woman who looked as pale and faded as the furniture. "She invited me to a party tomorrow night."

"That's nice, dear, very nice." Mrs. Banning sat up against her pillows and smiled vaguely at him. "I wish you could go to more parties, dear," she said.

She looked so defenseless, propped up there, her thin hands plucking at the afghan which covered her, that Paul closed his eyes to strengthen his resolve. Then he took a deep breath, opened them, and began, "Mother, I don't want you to be hurt by what I'm going to say, and I don't want you to think that I want to leave you. I don't. But I can't stay here any longer."

"Oh, son."

"I haven't any life here. I don't have any at Grandmother's, either, for that matter. I can't have my friends come—I can't go out. Don't you see, Mother?" he pleaded, leaning over and taking her nervous hand in his. "I have to start making a place for myself in the world. I'm young," he said. "I may live fifty or sixty years more. I have to start thinking about what I'll *be* during those years. You don't want me to be like the rest of the Bannings, do you?"

"No, Paulie."

"I would be. I'd be a crackpot for sure." He laid her hand against his cheek and said earnestly, "I'm not blaming you, Mother, please don't think I am—but it's terrible here. What kind of a Christmas did we have? I almost couldn't answer when Cinda asked me. What if I'd told her that my father walked downstairs and handed me three shares of stock? Three shares of stock and a lecture. 'Take care of it, Paul. The income from it will be small, but remember this: money, once spent, never comes back.' "

"He knows it only too well, dear. That little bit of stock was all he had to give you."

"He could have gone in town and bought me a fountain pen and a pair of shoes; you did. And he could have tied them up with tissue paper and red ribbon."

"Paulie, listen." She leaned over and stroked his hair with her free hand as she said carefully, "I have no right to tell you this, because I promised your father a long time ago that I never would—not until he was ready to tell you, himself. But I can't let you go on misjudging your father so, Paul. He hasn't any money. Not any. It's gone. Don't condemn him too harshly."

He sat looking past her as if he hadn't heard, but she knew he had, for he asked, "How long ago?"

"Ten years, at least."

He thought of the cracked swimming pool, the unkempt lawn, except for the little flower garden his mother loved and tended, the fraying furniture, the inadequate kitchen. He thought, too, of the gay resorts his father had taken his family to, the trips to Europe, the lavish living in this big house when it was new. And he remembered the tales his grandmother constantly repeated about his father as a young man at Princeton, owning only imported cars and throwing away more money on the races and costly junkets to New York than most students spent on their whole educations. It seemed that the Bannings had paid dearly for a spoiled only son.

"And I suppose Grandmother won't come up with another nickel to help us," he said aloud. "Oh no. She has to sit in her mausoleum, remembering the good old days, while two servants wait on her."

His mother sighed. "She doesn't have her fortune, Paulie. Your grandfather and your father were very poor investors. They didn't mean to be," she defended, "but they were. And Celeste and André are old, now, and need a home. They work for almost nothing."

"And so here we sit, the Bannings, poor but proud." Paul dropped her hand and flung himself out of his chair. "I hated my father because I thought he was stingy, but now I find he's only poor. Well, why doesn't somebody do something?" he railed, pacing up and down, then leaning against the mantel, his forehead in his hands. "Why doesn't he sell this run-down show place for the mortgage, or subdivide it, the way other people are doing, and move to town and get a job? Any kind of job, where you wouldn't be sick and tired out from working yourself to death? Why doesn't my grandmother auction off that mess of paintings and silver, and the dishes General Washington's supposed to have eaten from? She and Grandfather could live for years on the money they'd bring. And she could turn her house into apartments, and get good rent for them; and she could let you have one and could share her rickety servants with you. What's the matter with them all?"

"They're Bannings, Paul. They don't know any other way to live."

"And I'm a Banning, too, don't forget. What kind of a Banning am I supposed to be," he demanded, "with three shares of stock for a college education?" He scrubbed his forehead with the heel of his hand, then went over and dropped to his knees beside the sofa. "Mother," he said tenderly, "I know everything I say hurts you. I know you've done the best you could and wrecked yourself trying, but your way isn't my way. I can't lie down under it and become another crackpot, just because I'm a Banning. Don't you see? I haven't anything to fall back on. I've got to make my own way."

"Yes, Paulie, but not until after you finish school. I thought—perhaps . . ."

"It has to be *now*, Mother." He sat down on the floor beside her, long legs crossed, his arms around her, as he told her proudly, "I've already got a job. Two jobs, really. I'm going to jerk sodas in the drugstore from four to nine, with Friday night and most of Saturday off. And our physics teacher has offered me a room at his house for sitting with his kids on Friday nights, and cleaning up the joint on Saturdays. He wants me to be a physicist, and I'll learn a lot from living with him. He's a swell guy and his wife's nice, too. He thinks I've got a lot of promise."

"Oh, darling, I can't bear the thought of that."

Slow tears rolled down Mrs. Banning's cheeks, and as he wiped them tenderly away, Paul said, "It's better than living the way I do, now, unhappy and lonesome all the time. I'll come home sometimes, Mother, and it'll do you good to come in and see me. I'll make you the swellest chocolate soda you ever tasted, and I'll take you to the movies, and we'll have such a lot to talk about."

"But, oh, Paul, to work your way through school!"

She turned her face into the pillow, away from him, but he brought it back and said with a grin, "I'd have to work my way through college, even if I got a scholarship. It's no disgrace to work; loads of fellows do it. And they turn out to be a whale of a lot better business men than the Bannings."

He hoped she would smile with him, but she covered her eyes with her thin fingers, and said under them, "I don't know, Paul. I don't know about anything."

"You want me to be happy, don't you?"

"You know I do. I've worried so. I hated the thought of your being so shut in, but there seemed to be nothing I could do about it." She took her hands down and laid them on each side of his young face. "You're such a good son," she sighed.

"And you're such a dear, good mother."

She *was* good; but she was weak. And patting gently, watching her poor face twitch, he admitted to himself, So would I be, if I'd had to put in as many years being bossed as she has. I was pretty weak when I met Cinda. I hadn't really begun to make any plans. That's when I found out what a real home ought to be.

"You know what I think I'll do?" he said, wanting to be companionable and close. "I think I'll fix us some supper, and you'll be a lady while I do it. And I'll light a roaring fire in the fireplace, and we'll eat in here. And while we eat, I'll tell you about a girl."

"Paul?" she asked, holding him as he started to get up. "You won't go away from me forever, will you?"

"You bet I won't. I'll come to see you every week that you don't come to see me," he promised lightly. "And I'll bring you a box of candy, and I'll look so prosperous you won't know me. My coat and pants will match."

"Your father isn't going to approve of it."

"Oh, I guess he will, someday—when the magazines have printed my success story. Until then," he dropped a kiss on her nose, and said as he unfolded himself, "you keep out of the row. It's going to be a lulu, but you let me be the one to tell the old man that his son's going into the drugstore business. You play innocent."

"And now, *Madame*," he asked, making a creaking bow, almost as stiff as old André's, "will you have pheasant under glass or settle for creamed chipped beef and scrambled eggs, which I do much better?"

"Anything you say."

She watched him hobble away, his hand to his back, where André put his when his rheumatism bothered him, and felt sadder and prouder than she had ever felt in her life.

Out in the kitchen, Paul got out a skillet and opened and closed the refrigerator door. Nothing had been changed, really. A penurious man had become, by just a few halting words, a poor one. He was still arrogant, still a gentleman farmer of sorts, still falsely proud. He would still compute the extra cost of keeping the hired man on week ends, and would refuse to see where bus fares, lunch money, and the small allowance he had been doling out would more than pay it. He would rant and rave. But, breaking eggs into a bowl, Paul felt free.

His decision was made, his first step taken. It was like starting off on a long, long road that tapered off to a point on the horizon. He had walked the first mile, now, and while the road still stretched endlessly ahead, he could see a little farther along it. He had told his mother.

Standing at the stove, tearing up pieces of dried beef and dropping them into a pan of hot milk, he began a wonderful daydream. Someday, so far along that road that he couldn't see it yet, there would be a lovely life for his mother; a little house, perhaps, near the big laboratory where he would work, with other young physicists dropping in for chats around the fire. A little car in the garage. Just a nice, sturdy little car, instead of the longest station wagon on wheels. He couldn't fit his father into the picture, not anywhere, although he tried. So he let his mother drive home to see him now and then. She drove the way she used to when he was a little boy on the seat beside her, laughing and letting her hair blow in the wind, but carefully, too.

Everything was up to him, he thought, scrambling eggs, buttering toast, setting a glass dish of strawberry preserves on a big, silver tray. He took out and put back the huge damask napkins his father was accustomed to using and didn't have to iron, and laid two paper ones beside the knives and forks. Then he served his plates and put his pans to soak in the sink.

"*Madame*, dinner is served," he announced, turning into a young André under his heavy load. "A seat by the fire for *Madame*, perhaps?"

"*Merci*." His mother smiled at the quick way he set his tray on the floor, took magazines and a cigarette box from a small table, dumped them down, too, and put the table in front of a wingchair, the tray on it.

"There you are," he said, touching a match to well-laid logs in the fireplace. "Cozy, huh?"

"Will you do me the honor of dining with me?" she asked, crossing the room and letting him seat her with a flourish.

"Ah, *Madame*, an uncouth fellow like me? Well, thanks!"

He sat on the floor before the fire and reached up for his plate. "This is my idea of comfort," he said, having decided to keep the conversation on a light gay track. "You know that girl I said I'd tell you about? Well, her name's Cinda Hollister. I like her a lot."

"I know her parents."

"Her mother said you do." He took a few bites and launched forth, "They're a swell family. They were all trimming the tree and whooping it up the other night when I stopped by. Oh, by the way," he tossed off, "I took her a box of candy."

"I'm glad you did, dear."

"A darn big box, charged against my wages," he laughed. "Oh, well. And Cinda calls her mother 'Moth.' Don't you think," he looked up to ask, "it's a sort of nice, informal name for a mother?"

"It sounds companionable," she agreed. "I like it."

"Well, Moth," he went on, grinning and trying it out for size, "that's where the party's to be. I'm going to spend the night with her brother—that's Jinx, but his real name's Lindsey—and we're going skating tomorrow, only I haven't owned any skates for years. Marty O'Conner's brothers ought to have some around, though. Or Jinx and I can take turns."

He seemed unperturbed by his skateless status, and they went on talking companionably together while the fire burned lower and lower. Mrs. Banning even grew brave enough to suggest asking his three friends in for a cup of tea before they went on to the O'Conners'; and when the logs had settled into a dull glow of embers, he said reluctantly, "Here goes for the dishes. I have to get up early and do all the chores alone, you know."

It was the nearest he had come to mentioning his father all evening. They had talked of his childhood, of things they had done together, but always remembering the good times in which only they two had shared: hunting nuts in the woods, riding along country lanes, he on a fat brown pony, she on a chestnut hunter; a circus they had seen, a snow fort they had made. And they had laughed together over his first day in kindergarten, when he had refused to leave unless he could take his little chair home with him.

She was lovely when she laughed. And doing the dishes together, he realized how seldom her face had twitched tonight; and he silently vowed to come home and spend a night with her, whenever his father was away. What a pity, he reflected, that his father went away so seldom.

"Good night, Moth," he said at the foot of the stairs. "I'll put up the fire screen and turn out the lights."

"Good night, Paulie, darling," she answered, kissing him. "It's been such a lovely evening."

He watched her go up, too stooped for her age, then made everything safe, and hurried up after her.

His room was, or had been, beautiful. Wine-colored spreads with large gray monograms, carefully mended and darned, covered the twin beds, wine-colored curtains had been dyed again and again. The gray rug, once so thick that its pile had been deep enough to cuddle around a boy's bare toes, had lost most of its nap; and the wallpaper was faded into an indistinct pattern.

Paul took a suitcase out of the closet and opened it on a bed. A few shirts, a pair of clean pajamas, two neckties, shorts, socks, and an undershirt were all he had to put in it. His summer dressing gown was too faded to take, and he couldn't risk going to his grandparents for his wool one, until after he was settled in at Mr. Thompson's.

"Then I'll simply march in and pack up," he told himself, going to the closet for his new black shoes. "Only I bet I won't. It's going to be rugged, and I may have to sneak my clothes out."

He took his blue jacket and gray slacks from a hanger and stood holding them against him. They were freshly pressed, and he wanted to go down the hall and thank his mother. But she wouldn't like it. She always wanted him to think they had just come back from the cleaner's. With a sigh, he folded them carefully into the case, then snapped the lid shut.

It was still dark when he struggled out of bed and slipped into jeans and a flannel work shirt. The great barns were silent, the expensive cattle looked pensively at him above their stall bars, the three littlest calves peeking out below them. He fed them, opened the door for the big bull who had his own private play yard, shooed the cows and calves into several well-fenced pastures, and began shoveling out the bedding and replacing it with fresh. Fifty fine, fancy stalls to clean. One cow to find and lead back in again, ready for her buyer to claim her. Medicine to minister to a half-grown calf that mooed plaintively, complaining that he had a pain somewhere.

The sun came up and climbed higher and higher while Paul worked. Time was going too fast. He had less than half an hour in which to shower and change into his heavy cords and skating shirt. One more trough to fill with hay, one more pail of water . . . He looked up to see his father standing in the door.

"Your mother tells me," his father said, "that you're going to town."

"That's right, sir," Paul answered. "I'm going to a party. I wasn't sure when you'd be home, so I finished up everything I could. I guess it looks O.K."

"What time will you be back?"

"I won't be back."

They looked much alike as they faced each other: Paul a little taller, more slender, but no straighter. "I have a job in Glenvale, Father," he said, "so I'll be working full time until school starts again. After that, I plan to live at my physics teacher's. I can get ahead faster that way, and it won't cost you any money."

"Money!" His father shouted. "Who has been talking to you about money? Has your mother?"

"A blind man can see you're hard up," Paul answered, trying to keep his answer satisfactory but indefinite, by skirting the question. And to keep his father from asking it again, he said quickly, "I've been doing some thinking, and I've decided it's time for me to get out on my own."

"I'm the one who will do the thinking around here," his father thundered, taking a step forward and shaking his fist. "I'm the boss of this place, and don't you forget it."

"No, sir. I don't." Paul set his pitchfork against the wall and said quietly, "I'll be eighteen next week. Well, I've finished the barn so I'm going to town now."

He walked past his father, almost expecting the fist to swing in his direction, but not flinching. It was too late to argue further, even though his father shouted after him, "You can go to your party, but I expect you back here in the morning. Do you hear me? You come home in the morning!"

Paul walked steadily on.

"Everything's under control," he told his mother in the kitchen, glad she couldn't hear how hard his heart was pumping. "He doesn't know that you told me about the money or that I told you I'm moving out."

"He isn't angry?"

"He's as mad as hops." He gave her a pat, and called back as he hurried through the dining room, "But he'll get used to it. He'll have to. It's the only thing he can do."

He had ten minutes left for dressing, but he made it. His hair was still wet from the shower when he laid the three shares of stock on the dresser, grabbed his suitcase and charged down the stairs. "Good-by, Mother," he said, when he found her standing at the foot of the steps. "I'll call you tonight."

"But your friends, dear," she mentioned anxiously. "They haven't come yet, and I made the tea and some little cakes. We were going to ask them in, remember?"

"We can't, now, Mother. You see—well, there isn't much time." He couldn't hurt her by telling her his father had come home unexpectedly and ruined her fine plan; so he stumbled on, "They're later than I thought they'd be, so—well, I guess I'd better meet them down by the gate."

"All right, Paulie."

She nodded at him too brightly; and he let his suitcase bang to the floor and caught her in his arms. "Oh, I love you, Mother. I love you so much," he whispered, kissing her gently on the cheek. "Someday you'll understand. Then you'll be glad, Mother, I promise you, you will."

"I'm glad, now, darling. You're still my boy," she said, pulling back and smiling at him, "whether you live with your grandparents or that nice Mr. Thompson. I won't lose you. Now, run along."

He gave her one more hug, then picked up his suitcase. "I'll call you tonight if I get a chance, or in the morning, early. I'll call you every day that I can. And I'll be out to see you, and you'll come in . . ."

"Why, you're only going to a party, darling. Don't be so worried."

"O.K." He ran down the stone steps and stopped to look back at her and wave. "Good-by, Moth," he called. "I'll see you in a few days."

"Good-by, son."

She pressed her face against the glass and watched him go off down the long lane. His big hand clutched his suitcase, his fair hair ruffled up in the breeze, his big, heavy shoes tramped along. But he was still her little boy. Starting off to make his own future, he looked so young and lonely.

Chapter IX

CINDA laid the last package of sandwiches on the kitchen counter top, put twenty-two salad forks on a tray, twenty-two paper plates, and a whole box of paper napkins. Then she opened the refrigerator and checked the big bowl of fruit salad again, to be sure that Bobo hadn't been sampling it.

Working away, she remembered how disappointed she had been that morning, to find Paul standing on the shoulder of the road, making motions like a hitchhiker thumbing a ride. She was destined, it seemed, never to see inside the houses where he lived. But when they were skating around Marty's bumpy pond, not too gracefully, with their arms crossed for support, as first one then the other stubbed a skate on ripples a wind had frozen into the ice, Paul had said, "I'll be living at Thompsons' from now on and working in Peterson's. How about making the nine-thirty movie tomorrow night?"

"Well, my goodness, you certainly are casual about it," she had answered, stroking along. "First you told me you were going to have a horrible fight with your father, and worried me half to death; now you calmly announce that you're changing your address. Did you have the fight?"

"Not yet. I made an announcement, you might say. The fight will come later, and will probably drag on for months—until I go off and get a summer job, somewhere." He felt it only fair to let his father remain a wealthy man, since he wanted it that way, so he simply said, "I have to start saving for college, you know."

"Oh, I have a wonderful idea!"

She had been so busy looking at him that her skate struck an imbedded stick. And though she floundered along for a few jerky steps, she eventually went down and took him with her. "How about getting a job at the shore this summer?" she asked, just as if they were still gliding nicely, not sprawled on the ice. Then she sat up and hugged her knees. "College boys make simply scads of money, waiting table, down there," she said, "with a salary and tips. And you get your board and room, too."

"Gee, that's an idea."

"And you'd have time off between meals for some fun."

"And maybe I could bring Mother down for a week," he planned eagerly. "I could get her a room, somewhere."

"Why, she could stay right at our house!" Cinda cried, lavish with her mother's cottage and hospitality.

But he shook his head as he managed to get them both on their feet. "That's swell of you, but she'd better take a room. She isn't too well, you know." He had her upright and moving again; and as they took a long glide, he said, "I'll start looking into the job end of it right away. I suppose I should apply through an agency."

"Oh, you don't have to. Daddy knows all the men who run restaurants; and if Jinx can't get a lifeguard job, like War-Horse, he's going to be a bellhop in a hotel, because he's so awkward with dishes. I think," she had said proudly, "that I'm remembering how I used to skate backwards. If you'll turn me around and keep us out in the middle and watch for bumps, I'll try it. Oh, golly, this is fun!"

Now, finishing her last-minute preparations, with Stella and Down Boy listening to the radio in Stella's room, with Bobo safely at the movies with his parents, and with Buff and her best friend, Charmion Ayer, ready to dispose of the guests' coats and hats before they went upstairs for a slumber party that would have little slumber, she was faced with a dilemma. Listening to Charmion giggling in the coat closet had reminded her of it. Charmion was Melody's little sister.

"Help! Help!" she cried, charging into the library where Lindsey and Paula were sitting on the sectional divan, playing one of Buff's new Christmas games. "Somebody has to go and get Melody. Now that she and Page are mad at each other she hasn't a date, and she won't come by herself. I promised I'd send someone for her."

"Don't look at me." Lindsey spread a handful of picture cards, and said as he studied them, "Send Dick or War-Horse."

"You know they won't be here tonight, they've gone off on their own. Please, Jinx."

"I'm telling Paula's fortune. Put down a card, Paula."

Paula laid one on the cushion between them and said, laughing, "Charmion and Melody. Did you ever hear such names?"

"Oh, there are more." Cinda leaned over her to whisper, "There's Amanthis—she's married. And there's Gideon, who's away at college. Gideon, Amanthis, Melody, and Charmion." Then she straightened, and commanded, "Jinx Hollister, you get right up and go."

"I see a fine young man in your life," Lindsey went on with the fortune, studying his cards and paying no attention to her.

"He's built on the stocky side, very handsome—also athletic, powerful, charming."

"Oh, Lindsey, you don't." Paula pulled at the cards; and Cinda pulled, too.

"Jinx, I mean it!" Cinda cried. Then she let go, and asked, "Where's Paul?"

"He had a call to make, so I sent him upstairs to do it in peace." He looked at the bent cards, then held them face-out to Paula, and said, "As I live and breathe, he's the only guy in your life. You can look for yourself."

Cinda ran into the hall and met Paul just coming down the stairs. "I reversed the charges to Mother," he said. "She wanted me to tell you . . ."

"Here." She took an overcoat from the closet, saw Charmion sitting, stifflegged and expectant, on the floor beside Buff, and slammed the door on them. "You'll have to go," she whispered, dragging him away from alert little ears, "and pick up Melody. And you'll have to be especially nice to her all evening—unless Dick comes home early—which he said he won't."

"But I don't know her." Paul hated to protest doing whatever Cinda wanted him to do, but Melody Ayer was only a name to him. "She'll think I'm crazy."

"No, she won't. She'll be sitting there, practically with her coat on her lap. All you have to do," she explained, "is tell her you're our house guest. And when you get her here, just see that she's right in the middle of whatever's going on, in case Page should happen to look at her. I'll round up the rest of the gang to help you."

"Can't you ride over there with me?"

"Oh, that wouldn't do at all. Take Jinx's car, it's the only one out, and if Melody remarks that it isn't plushy as a Sunbeam, you can call attention to the new seat covers and tires. Now hurry and get out before the other cars start coming in."

She started him off and wondered, too late, if he knew where Melody lived. Oh, well, he'll find her, she thought, releasing her self-appointed maids as footsteps sounded on the porch.

Guests began arriving by twos, fours, even eight in Barbie Devereaux's station wagon. Charmion was completely useless because she got the giggles, and Buff made so many curtsies that she was always being pushed aside; so Cinda let the coats pile up on her own arms and introduced Paula from across them.

"You know where to go," she kept saying, motioning upward when she could, listening to the steady tramp and tapping of heels on the stairway, as everyone hurried up to the most popular room in Glenvale.

"Honestly!" she scolded, when she was left alone with sixteen coats and an assorted collection of scarves and mismated gloves. "You kids were no help at all. If you hadn't been here they'd have put their own things where they could find them."

"We tried, Cinda, we truly did," Buff answered. "I can't be polite and grab at the same time. That scarf," she said, pointing, "belongs with the fur coat. I know exactly what everybody wore, so if you'll just go away I'll fix things."

"You'd better."

Another car pulled in, far down on the very end of the line, and Cinda waited to receive Paul and her most difficult guest. There was no knowing how Melody might behave. She was a pretty little thing, with enormous eyes in a small square face. Her narrow shoulders and tiny waist suggested a Dresden figurine, and she looked quite breakable. Mr. and Mrs. Ayer always treated Melody as something precious. But it was Page who popped in when she opened the door.

"Oh, dear, I'd forgotten you weren't here, yet," she said, hoping to hustle him upstairs. "Give Buff your coat and come on."

"What's the rush?"

He laid his heavy driving gloves on the fireside bench, carefully folded his cap and put it in his pocket, unwound enough muffler to wrap a Maypole, quite oblivious to Buff's bobs, or Cinda's waiting on the landing.

"I want to get the party going," Cinda urged, annoyed by his deliberation, but flattering him diplomatically. "You always liven things up."

She thought she heard a familiar motor give its dying cough out on the street. Allowing for the long walk in, she had about two minutes in which to get him upstairs and inconspicuously placed. If Melody were to arrive and find them receiving guests as a couple, the evening would be wrecked before it began. "Hurry," she said, and flitted up out of sight.

Page flung off his coat and followed so quickly, then, that Kitty Lou, dancing with her eyes watching the door, saw him come in behind Cinda's red dress, saw him in front of it, and saw him alone.

"Excuse me, sugah," she said to her partner, wondering what kind of a magic disappearing act Cinda had done, "I think my sandal's comin' off. I reckon I'd bettah go down an' fix it."

She hobbled across the floor, ran into Page as if she hadn't seen him, and apologized sweetly and without a change in tone, "Excuse me, sugah. I was goin' down to fix my sandal, but maybe you can tell me if I broke the heel or only twisted it a little." She took off the slipper, held it out to him and asked anxiously, "Did I break it, do you think?"

"It seems all right to me." Page looked at crossed straps that might have been made of clear glass, at a heel that might have been an icicle picked from a roof, and asked, "Can you dance in those things?"

"Oh, yes, they'ah my Cinderella slippahs." Kitty Lou slipped the sandal back on, and said, fluttering her lashes, "Did you mean you'ah askin' me to dance, now?"

"I guess so."

Someone had put on a mambo record, so he and Kitty Lou started off on the hardwood floor. She was a good dancer; and no matter how often he spun her around and let go of her, she always finished a whirl and was there to catch his hand again, always in step and following his lead. But she lacked the grace of Melody and the vivacity of Cinda. She simply danced in a rhythmic, practiced way. And she never wanted to stop.

He watched Cinda come up with Melody and that oaf from the country, take Melody over to the group surrounding Paula, and go back to the oaf. "Gosh, Kitty Lou," he said, "I'm out of breath, aren't you?"

"Not a bit."

Cinda and the oaf were dancing, now, he noticed, and he had to admit they were good. The big clod could cross his feet and tangle them around, then come out in a backstep and a forward shuffle that sailed Cinda under his arm, yet let him yank her back at the end of a twirl.

Lindsey was tangling his feet, too, as Page had so aptly put it, but not untangling them so expertly. He was lost from Paula more than he was with her; and finally they retired to sit on the sidelines. "This old house sure can take it," he said. "The first time we had a brawl up here, Mom ran all over the second floor, moving vases and taking down pictures. She was sure the ceilings were going to split wide open, but not a thing busted."

He glared at anyone who came near the old lawn bench where they rested, looking so fierce that no one dared join them. Paula seemed content. She listened to a waltz record Cinda put on, and asked idly, "Lindsey, are you going to Princeton next year?"

"Now, what made you ask me that?"

He turned his head, but she only smiled and shrugged. "I don't know," she said. "Something you wrote in your letters, I suppose. Something about Princeton being too fancy for your taste, too close to home, and—forgive me if I'm wrong, but I seemed to read between the lines—too much Warren's school. Am I right or wrong, Lindsey?"

"Partly some of each, I guess," he answered. "I wouldn't mind going to Princeton because of War-Horse. We don't compete in the same things, but I'd rather be in a school of my own. I went up to visit him, and the Joes were swell to me, but—well, I felt like his dumb little brother all the time I was there. I'm not the Ivy League type. I think I'd do better out west in a big university. Horace Greely said, 'Go West, young man, go West,' and I've been considering it."

Something in his words made her regard him intently. Lindsey never had told her directly that she was the only girl he liked, but she knew it. And she began to wonder if she might be the reason for this sudden pull toward a western university. "It would be wonderful if you'd come to Colorado U. or Colorado School of Mines," she said, offering bait for her curiosity instead of a questionnaire.

"Gosh, no." He gave his head such a vigorous shake that she was both surprised and puzzled. "I hadn't thought of going *that* far," he said. "Michigan, maybe. Michigan State, or perhaps Purdue, in Indiana. They're in the Big Ten."

Football, of course. His other love. "I might have known," she said, crinkling up her nose and laughing at her own vanity as much as at him. "Lindsey, did you know there's nobody anywhere who's as brutally honest as you are?"

"How come?"

"Why, anybody else would have said, 'Paula, I'd like to come out in your territory, but I can't make it that far. Oh, I wish I could, but I can't.' "

"Well, I can't. You see . . ." He took her hand and held it up, spreading the fingers. "Here are five good reasons why I can't," he said, turning the little finger down. "One, I wouldn't study if I could drive to Colorado Springs and see you every whipstitch. Two," another finger went down, "Colorado isn't tops in football. Three," he bent the third finger slowly as he said, "Colorado hasn't had me scouted. Four," the index finger stayed upright longer than the others, before he doubled it over and mumbled, "the coach hasn't written me a nice letter, telling me he'd like to have me try out for his squad and that he's sure his school is just the right spot for a man of my mental capabilities. Five . . ."

"Oh, Lindsey," she interrupted, really excited, now, "has Michigan State?"

"Yeah, several colleges have. It doesn't mean too much," he stated flatly. "Just that they're interested. Lots of fellows get letters."

"But it sounds so important. Doesn't your father think so?" she asked.

"Dad? We haven't said too much. He knows I'm no brain, and he wants me to go where I won't wash out. He's not sure his little boy, Lindsey, can keep his head in a big university. He'd rather I'd go to one of the smaller, midwest colleges for a year or two."

"Have any of those asked you?"

"Oh, sure. A friend of Dad's went to Wabash, and has been yaking at me; and there's a guy from Depauw. You might say I'm playing the field."

"Oh, Lindsey, what fun!"

"Or I might go South. Duke's O.K.. Maryland and Penn State have good teams, but they're a little too close to home."

The world was his oyster. Paula couldn't think of a single person whom she would rather have open it and find a pearl inside. She was about to tell him so when Paul walked purposefully across the room and offered in rueful apology.

"Sorry, but Cinda says I have to break this up, Jinx. She wants you to start table tennis going. How about dancing, Paula?"

"I'd love to."

They took a few steps, then he slowed and said with a shy smile, "Cinda's been making quite a lot out of our names. She thinks we should have some sort of affinity or secret attraction for each other because of it. Has she talked to you about it?"

"Oh, goodness, yes."

He had one of the nicest smiles Paula had ever watched. It grew slowly, as if unsure just how big it should be, then let loose and lit up his whole face. She liked to study smiles. Lindsey's started and ended in a happy grin; Warren's flashed and was gone; Cinda's was quick, gay, and usually followed by a barely audible chuckle. "I think," she said, answering this one with lips that curved beautifully and scarcely changed the contour of her cheeks, "she's hoping to hear the wedding service read. 'I, Paul, take thee, Paula.' She says it would be so romantic."

They both laughed and looked at Cinda, marking time and listening to Page. His arm was about her waist, her left hand rested lightly on his shoulder and she absentmindedly fingered her necklace with her right. "I think you are being awfully silly," they heard her say as they danced past. "Melody didn't mean to get off the train with Stephen Elston, and you know it. He sat down beside her and started talking, that's all."

"Who cares?" his answer followed them. "Can't you get it through your crazy little head that I don't care at all?"

"But *I* do!" Her retort was as loud and emphatic as if she had spoken through a microphone. "Melody's utterly—I mean, she's *desolate*."

Melody looked anything but desolate at the moment. Dick had appeared at the top of the stairs and was heading straight for her. Paula watched him, then saw Warren come up, too, and missed a step.

"Sorry," she said, and picked up the beat again.

Somebody had started a conga line. It was winding around the tennis table, and she asked, a little confused and embarrassed, "Shall we join on?"

"If you want to."

Two hands broke apart to let them in, but Cinda tweaked Paul's blue jacket. "I'm going down to get the food," she said, her cheeks pink. "Will you come with me?"

"Sure."

Lindsey had pushed into Paul's place in the line, so he followed her down the stairs.

Her red skirt fluttered out in the air she stirred up, and when they reached the window on the lower landing, she stopped and exploded crossly, "It wouldn't do any good even to make a wish, right now. Honestly!"

She tapped down the last few steps and stopped in the hall to ask, "Wouldn't you think a party could go the way you want it to? Just once?"

"It looks like a pretty good party to me," he answered. "What's wrong with it?"

"Everything. I don't know why I thought Page Vandergren was such a dream boy. He's nothing but a—a wolf! And Kitty Lou's gone and shut herself up in War-Horse's room because she says Page insulted her, and she won't come out. And why did Dick and War-Horse have to show up when they said they *wouldn't!* I might have managed and got things straightened out," she sighed, "if they'd stayed away."

"Cinda, listen." Paul led the way to the kitchen and put both hands on her shoulders. "You can't make people fall for the ones you want them to," he said. "They're growing up."

"But not that much," she protested, her eyes somber as she looked up at him. "They ought to be young and have fun. Nobody should act so silly at our age: Kitty Lou crying, and Barbie clinging to Artie Green like half of a Siamese twin, and Paula coming unglued because War-Horse came home. Oh, I saw her!"

"Look." He piloted her to a chair by a table and pulled another one up before her. "Let's take 'em one at a time," he suggested, sitting down astride his and resting his arms on its back. "O.K.?"

"I guess so." She nodded.

"Let's take Page first. He's seventeen. He liked Melody for a while, and now he likes you."

"Oh, he doesn't!"

"And he may shift again tomorrow—just the way Melody's shifted to Dick. They aren't thinking of getting *married*, you know. And Paula likes both Jinx and Warren. I've watched her today, and I think she likes them equally much. She can have Jinx, but she isn't sure of Warren. People like the fun of a chase. Cinda, each one we've mentioned is after someone he or she can't have."

"Then I don't see how people ever get married."

She laughed a little, knowing it to be a silly conversation, but he only smiled the slow tentative grin Paula had liked, and said, "That comes along later. Some marry the wrong ones, but they usually marry."

"I don't think I ever will."

She gave such a hearty sigh that he smiled again and asked, "Don't you want to be like your mother and father, and have a home and a bunch of kids like theirs?"

"Well—perhaps," she conceded. "But years and years from now. Not until I have good sense."

"That's the way I figure it." He set his chair back and pulled her to her feet. "It'll be a long time off for me, too, I guess. I'll have to be financially able, first, and then I'll have to find the gal who think I'm just the guy for her. How about loading up some trays?"

"All right." She watched him unwrap and arrange sandwiches without having to be told how; and said sincerely and from the very depths of her heart, "You know, I don't think you'll have the least bit of trouble finding her, Paul."

Chapter X

"Did you ever give a party that turned out to be a total flop?" Cinda asked her mother, sliding her dustcloth across a a living room table and by-passing a lamp and magazines.

Mrs. Hollister was trying to make a dozen tired Christmas roses stand up and look lively, and she asked absently, "What was wrong with last night? It sounded noisy enough to me."

"Oh, it was *noisy*." Cinda moved half-heartedly on with her dusting, then sat down and hung her cloth between her knees. "I guess I was too excited about it, beforehand," she said. "I thought it was going to be such a smash."

"And wasn't it?"

"No! Almost everybody was mad, or hurt, or quarreling; and the few who weren't, held hands and smooched, right out there in plain view. Oh, things were pretty good sometimes," she said reflectively, "In the middle part, while we were eating, and right afterward. But it wasn't the way our parties used to be."

"What happened, specifically?" The roses refused to make a gallant effort, so Mrs. Hollister fed them some aspirin tablets and turned to devote herself to her woeful housemaid.

"Well, darn it," Cinda said, "it was mostly me, I guess, just me. Paul told me that. And Jinx blasted me for picking on Paula." She clamped her lips shut to take in a deep breath and let it out again, before she said, "I *didn't*, Moth! I simply said . . ."

Paula came running down the stairs. She wore her soft fur coat, and said breathlessly, "Cousin Frances, I was going to help Stella with the breakfast dishes, but Warren said he'd run me down town for a lipstick and some nail polish I need, if I could go right away. Will Stella wait 'til I come back, do you think?"

"Of course, child." Mrs. Hollister was not blind to the sparkle in Paula's eyes, nor deaf to the low "humph!" that came from Cinda. "Buff's earning an extra dime," she said, "so run along."

"Oh, thank you!" Paula was almost at the door before she remembered to call back and ask, "Don't you want to grab your coat and come, too, Cinda? Warren has his motor running, so hurry."

"I'll stick around here." Cinda listened to the door close, then glowered at her mother. "There! You see? That's what I mean about last night. She treated Jinx like dirt after War-Horse showed up. And she has a dozen lipsticks and wouldn't be caught putting so much as a drop of polish on her own nails."

Mrs. Hollister wished an aspirin could do as much for her daughter as it was doing for the roses. A loving heart needs just the right medicine to heal its ache, even if the ache is often imaginary, so she tried to find a sugar-coated pill that would do the work. "I think you're being too serious, dear," she said carefully. "Paula is here in a houseful of boys. She's excited, and having fun. She went skating with Lindsey yesterday, so why can't she go to town with Warren today?"

"That's just it." Cinda stood up and expounded, waving her dust cloth, "We used to do things together. We piled in the cars, all together. Down at the shore we swam together; and Jinx went where War-Horse went, and Paula went, too, and so did I. Now look at us!"

"I don't think you can do a thing about it." Her mother still remembered the youthful pains of growing up; so, loving one son as much as the other, she said, "Lindsey must work out his own problems, darling. He's Lindsey, so I'm sure he will."

"But he's so good. And War-Horse is so darned handsome. I love War-Horse," she defended, "and if any girl mistreated him I'd scratch her eyes out. But," and she sighed again, "no girl ever will. Paula won't, anyway. I wish Paula had stayed out in Colorado Springs where she belongs!"

"Cinda!"

"Well, I do." She gave a wry grin and said, "I'm just cross this morning. I'm cross with Paul's mean old father, and I could murder Melody Ayer for not getting off the train by herself, and I'm mad at Dick for showing up when I was about to get Melody and her wolf back together again. It looks as if I'd had a bad night, doesn't it?" she ended.

"Perhaps you'd better go up and help the boys clean the third floor," her mother suggested. "Paul was running the vacuum and Lindsey the waxer, when I came down."

"They're almost through by now, I guess."

It was a cantankerous morning. Cinda dropped her cloth and hurried up to offer her services on the third floor, where the roommates were becoming good friends and carrying on a conversation above the whirr of their motors and Dick's whistle in the tower room.

"If you like it here," Lindsey yelled, while Cinda stopped on the steps to listen, "I don't see any reason why you should move in at the Thompsons' until school starts again. They don't expect you, and I've got that extra bunk."

"But wouldn't your mother mind?" Paul shouted back.

"Gosh, no. She never knows how many we have around. When we run out of places at the table, somebody eats in the kitchen."

"I'll be working all day. Well, if she says it's O.K., thanks, a lot."

The waxer stopped whirring its brush, and Lindsey suggested, "How about us driving over to your grandparents' and getting your gear?"

"Think it looks shipshape up here?"

"Aye, matey."

Paul shut off his vacuum cleaner, too; and Cinda ran up the rest of the way to make her presence known. "I came up to help," she said in a hesitant voice.

"We've just finished." Lindsey swung the waxer over his shoulder, and offered as a great favor, "You can bring the trash basket down with you. Come on, Paul, let's get going."

They marched down in close formation; and although Cinda was the middle marcher, Lindsey ignored her while he made plans over his shoulder, so she fell out when they passed her room.

I don't see why I got so steamed up about him, she thought gloomily, standing beside her window and watching him stop beside his car to clap a hand on Paul's shoulder. He's quite a manager.

She felt mistreated. Paul was *her* protegé. If anyone accompanied him to the house on Cedar Lane and forcefully wrested his wardrobe from his grandparents, she should be the one. Lindsey would get to see the gold chairs and the ballroom. He would, she thought, if he had sense enough to ask to, which he probably wouldn't. Lindsey didn't know a drawing room from a library, or a gold chair from a kitchen stool.

The idea suddenly amused her, just as it would have yesterday morning, and her grumpiness vanished. I'm the one who's been out of step, she realized reluctantly. Moth tried to tell me that. I should have said to Paula, "Sure I want to go, so wait for me." And I could have asked Jinx and Paul, "What's wrong with taking me along?" I'm making dire situations out of nothing at all. Well!

She put on a fresh white blouse and a green cardigan to match her skirt, and ran down the stairs. "I wish," she said, flying past the landing window and sliding her finger across a diamond almost as large as the Kohinoor, "that Cinda Hollister would quit acting like a creep. I wish, too," she ran back to request of a large sapphire, "that somebody would come back and get me."

With two wishes made and her day in focus again, she proceeded to a living room window and framed her face in a holly wreath. Someone would surely come back.

Paula and Warren had no intention of being the ones. They had paid for a nickel's worth of parking time before the ten cent store and were having an argument.

"I think you're crazy," Warren was saying. "You're having a good time here with us, so why should you want to meet your folks in New York and hole up in a hotel?"

"I wouldn't call staying at the Waldorf Astoria exactly 'holing up,'" Paula returned haughtily. "And besides, I told you that Mother and Daddy Fred said I could invite you and Lindsey to have dinner with us and go to the theater, and to the Stork Club, or any night spot we'd like to see. They said I could have Cinda stay there with us, if I want to."

"And what happens to our house party at home?" Warren

leaned back and rested his hands on the wheel, as he said, "Listen, chum. I go to college at Princeton. I'm so near New York that I can go up every week end, if I like. It so happens—I don't like. The debutantes in New York are crying for Princeton men, Yale men, and Harvard men—if they can make it that far—to come to their parties. All a fellow has to do is belong to a club, own a dinner jacket and white tie and tails, meet one girl, and he's on the list. I went up a few times, and I've seen enough of New York."

"I haven't." Paula thrust out her haughty little chin and said, "I'm from the wild and woolly west, you know. I haven't made a debut so naturally I'm not bored or blasé. I don't have a list of eligible young men to sit in my box at the opera, and be photographed with me in a night club. I only have a couple of good friends with whom I wanted to share some fun. I know, now, it was a mistake, but I hadn't heard how popular you are."

"Oh, cut it out." He frowned at her before he admitted grudgingly, "I suppose I did sound like a big wheel bragging, but I didn't mean it that way. I was just trying to make you see that it's a lot more fun to run in and out of our house than to ride up and down in an elevator, and that the New Year's dance at our club has the Starlight Roof knocked into a cocked hat. For me, that is. Perhaps you'd like the other better."

"I think I ought to find out," she retorted icily. "Lindsey might like it, too. He's not as grand as you are. He's a nice, simple, country boy."

"I wouldn't be too sure."

Warren wondered what he could say to correct the untrue picture he had drawn of himself, and at the same time paint a portrait of Jinx that would make him look like a man of mystery. Jinx was about as mysterious as Down Boy. And Paula was such a pretty girl, he thought, looking across at her. She was too coolly detached and lacking in warm, human companionship for his taste, but she seemed to suit Jinx. Jinx had enough human warmth to heat Alaska.

"Jinx and I don't think alike in lots of ways," he said cautiously, "but I guess I know him pretty well. He's a small-town fellow—you're right about that—but I suppose he has more reason to be than I have."

"Why?" she asked, falling neatly into his trap. "Because of his athletics?"

"Partly." He turned on the seat and gave her the full flash of his grin. "I guess you didn't know you wrecked the hopes of a couple of gals by coming for Christmas, did you?" he said lightly. "One took the job of cheer leader so she could be out on the field, near the team. And the other one, the little red-headed kid who was here last night, thought she stood tops until you showed up. Mom stews about the way they keep telephoning Jinx, but I told her not to worry—he'll be going off to college, next year. As a football player," he added, proud of the hidden meaning in that last subtle appendage.

Paula caught it. "If you think you're going to make me writhe with jealousy," she said, "you're wrong. I know Lindsey just as well, if not better, than you do. You were the one who labeled him Jinx when he was a little boy, because you didn't want him with you and said he always made everything go wrong when you took him. *I* don't call him Jinx. I call him Lindsey."

"Good for you." He patted her hand, but she drew away from him.

"And he told me all about the 'two cute little idiots,' as he calls them, and about going to a midwestern college. He tells me everything; and there's only one trouble."

"What's that?"

"We're almost the same age, yet I feel as if I'm older than he is." She looked out at the cold shoppers hurrying along the sidewalk, and said honestly, "I don't want to feel that way, but I do. Perhaps having my father die when I was little, then living with women for fifteen years, with Mother, and Grandmother, and Aunt Maud, made me look at everything from an older viewpoint, I don't know. I don't want to—but sometimes I find myself talking down to Lindsey."

"Oh, Paula, you shouldn't. He's a grand guy."

"I know that. Well," she opened the car door, and said, "I won't be but a minute." Then she stood on the pavement and added unhappily, her blue eyes wistful, "This isn't the talk I meant to have with you, Warren. I was going to invite you to New York and show you how attractive I can be, and—and what a lot of fun. But it wouldn't have worked, would it?"

"I guess not, Paula. I like you, right here. Jinx does, too," he added.

He watched her go into the store, then scowled at his reflection in the rearview mirror. "Gosh, darn it," he growled, "I do like the kid. I meant that. But why does she have to push it?" He flung his hands out in a hopeless gesture, dropped them to the wheel, and sat in morose gloom.

Paula came back with a flat little paper bag that looked too small to hold a guarantee for "kissable lips" and enough red lacquer to paint ten nails twenty-two times. He leaned over to open the door for her, and asked as he started his motor, "Anything else you have to do?"

"No, I just want to go home and tell Cousin Frances about Mother's letter and that I'll be going to New York day after tomorrow. She—she doesn't know it, yet."

They were embarrassed to look at each other. They would

have to avoid each other all the rest of today and tomorrow, one fleeing to another room when the other came in, unless they talked the thing out. So Warren said uncomfortably, "Listen, Paula. You're seventeen—well, almost eighteen," he corrected, as her lips parted, "I'm twenty. I've got a long time ahead of me before I ever get serious about a girl. About *any* girl," he emphasized, "you, or anyone else. Maybe I could fall for one, but I'm not trying. Jinx—Lindsey—is different. A girl can help him get where he wants to go. You're the girl he's picked, so, with things as they are . . ."

"You don't have to explain all this, Warren," she interrupted, her head high, her lips holding a determined smile. "I didn't mean that I was in *love* with you."

"You didn't?"

"Why, of course, not." Warren had had his turn; and since people can be made to believe whatever they want to believe, she told him untruthfully, "I think of you as a brother, just as Cinda does. I always look up to you and think you know more that the rest of us. And if I explained about feeling older than Lindsey, and not caring as much for him as—as everyone says he cares for me, it was because I wanted you to understand, and—and—perhaps help me a little. You see," she said haltingly, "I—I don't want to get too serious, either."

"Oh." He was able to look at her, now. Her beautiful eyes were close to his and reflecting his own image, as he said, "That's great, Paula. You sort of fooled me for a few minutes. You had me scared."

"Girls can always fool men." She laughed and leaned back, her funny little package on her lap; and with a grin of relief, he backed the car out.

Cinda grabbed them in the hall when they came in, and inquired indignantly, "My soul, where were you? That silly old sapphire's not a bit of good, and I'll never wish on it again. I've waited twenty whole minutes!"

"Well, we're back," Paula answered, wishing they weren't. "What would you like to do?"

"I'd like to see the inside of Paul's grandmother's house," Cinda answered promptly. "But I can't."

"How would you like to go up to New York, instead, and stay in a hotel with me?" Paula asked.

"Huh?"

"With Mother and Daddy Fred and me, I mean." Mrs. Hollister had come up the basement stairs, and Paula went to her and asked eagerly, "Cousin Frances, Mother and Daddy Fred are coming to New York for a few days, so could Cinda go up with me, and stay in the hotel?"

"Why, gracious, I don't know. I'd have to have time to consider it," Mrs. Hollister answered, looking past her to see what signal Cinda might be sending.

Cinda's brow was furrowed, her eyes squinted almost shut and slightly crossed; so she searched frantically for a reason for refusal—any reason. "Well," she began, wondering what would come next, "I'd rather she wouldn't go, just now. She—I have a houseful, you know, and she does help me, some."

Cinda remembered her dispirited dusting, and felt inspired to sigh, "Poor Moth, I haven't put my shoulder to the wheel, as the saying goes. I'd really love to go to New York, Paula, but there's that blasted Christmas tree to take down, and Stella's been promised New Year's Day off, and the day after. I don't see how I could do it. Why don't you stay here?"

She looked as if she were about to set forth on a splurge of house cleaning; and Paula, who knew how allergic she was to a broom at the shore, how she could rise above the clutter in her dresser drawers for weeks on end, said knowingly, "All right, you can stay home. I have to go and meet my parents, though."

Warren had hung his coat away and was reaching back for hers. "I'm going to New York," she said, ignoring him and keeping it on. "I want to go," she added, sure he would understand, and feeling spitefully catty, "because Daddy Fred has a lot of wealthy friends in New York, who have sons. I'm sure they all go to college and own dinner jackets, so—if Daddy Fred pays the bills—we ought to have a wonderful time." Then she whirled and ran upstairs.

Chapter XI

PAULA was laying her dresses in the large but light case she had brought on the plane. "Daddy Fred told me I could buy a lot of new things in New York," she said, as Cinda handed her a belt that belonged to a fur-trimmed suit she hadn't yet worn. "I suppose Mother and I'll go on shopping tours every morning."

Cinda wondered what Paula could possibly want with more clothes, then decided that social life in Colorado Springs must be much dressier than in Glenvale, and remarked, "Then it's a good thing I'm not going with you. I'd have been green with envy, just sitting in stores and watching you try things on."

"Oh, I wouldn't shop at all if you'd stay up there," Paula was quick to answer. "I'd planned lots of lovely things for us to do if . . ." She stopped, then said wistfully, "I'd planned a hundred things between the time I read Mother's letter and the time Warren told me the whole idea was silly. Well," she sighed, "I guess he knew what he was talking about. You didn't want to go, either."

"I *did* want to go," Cinda asserted, "sort of. Or rather, I wanted you to stay here. Christmas vacation is such a lot of fun when we're all together, and I wanted you to share it. Didn't you have a good time here?" she asked anxiously.

"Oh, yes, I loved it. I truly did," Paula insisted, bending over the case. "But I can't disappoint Daddy Fred."

"Jinx is disappointed." Cinda wished Paula would turn around so they could talk face to face. "Jinx counted terribly on the New Year's dance, and having you drive down to the shore with him. Now that he has his new tires, he's going down to check on the cottages, and he thought you could look at yours and make a report to your father on it."

"I'm awfully sorry I can't do it." Paula turned around at last, to say slowly, "I'm not much interested in the cottage just now, because I won't be at the shore, next summer."

"*You won't be at the shore!*" Cinda was about to pass along a white net dress, but she sat down on a chair and clasped it to her. "Well, mercy me!" she cried. "Why won't you?"

"Because . . . oh, dear." Paula had hoped not to mention summer plans to Cinda. She had hoped to have no unusual ones to mention.

For the two summers since her mother and step-father had been married, they had come to the cottage he had bought on a small island off the Jersey coast. It was an accepted fact. As soon as June burst into glorious bloom on the mountains in Colorado, they drove East to a blue, rolling ocean that spilled its lace-trimmed breakers over a sandy beach. By mid-June, the Island's newspaper always carried the announcement, *Mr. and Mrs. Frederick Aldrich, and their daughter, Miss Paula Marsh, have opened their cottage, Sea Shingles, for the summer.*

"Oh, I might as well tell you," Paula said unhappily, pushing the case back and sitting down on the side of the bed. "Daddy Fred and Mother are going to Europe this summer. They went once before, you know, on their wedding trip, when I acted so awful because Mother had married again. Mother couldn't enjoy it because of worrying about me, so they came back. Remember?"

Cinda remembered only too well. Paula and her aunt had

lived in Grandmother Hollister's cottage at the shore, and Paula had been so jealous of her new step-father that she had kept everyone in an uproar. Cinda was still thinking about that worrisome summer, when Paula said gratefully:

"If it hadn't been for you, I'd never have known how wonderful Daddy Fred is, or what a selfish little beast I was. When he and Mother came back, and you liked him so much that you coached him on exactly how to make me like him . . . why, Cinda, it was the most wonderful thing anyone ever did! I've never really thanked you for it."

"You didn't need to."

"And Daddy Fred's such a darling! I can't do enough for Daddy Fred."

"Does he want you to go to Europe with them?"

"He left it up to me. I can either go with them or stay with Aunt Maud in the cottage." Paula looked down at her hands, rubbed one finger over a bright red thumbnail, studied it and rubbed it again, before she said, "I thought I'd come and visit you and decide."

"I don't see how visiting us could make you know whether you wanted to go, or not," Cinda said bluntly. "It seems to me you'd either want to go to the shore or go to Europe."

"I wasn't sure." Paula got up and became busy with her case again. "Daddy Fred often has business in Europe, and he said that if I don't want the trip for a graduation present, I can go some other time. We've always had such fun at the shore."

"And now you think we won't? What's to stop us?"

"Lots of things."

Only the white net dress was left to pack, and she took it from Cinda and ruthlessly mashed it on top. "There," she said, closing the lid.

Cinda sat and watched her. Something had happened between Paula and War-Horse, she decided, on that ride to town. They had spoken scarcely a dozen words to each other since then. And there was Paula's strange remark to remember, the one about having a good time with college boys in New York, and paying the check. And the casual good-by War-Horse had tossed off, at breakfast.

"Good-by, Coz," he had said, going around to her place at the breakfast table and lightly kissing her cheek. "Sorry I have a bowling date and have to leave so early. It's been fun having you here."

"I've had a wonderful time." Paula had reached up to take Dick's hand, and Paul's, then had gone on eating her breakfast. At least she had made a pretense of doing it. Thinking back, now, Cinda remembered that she had set a very tasty plate on the rug for Down Boy.

"I wish you'd change your mind," she said, wanting the old life to go on as it had. Then, to make Paula feel happier about her choice, she added, "I can't blame you for wanting to see Paris and London, and cathedrals and museums. Not to mention the fun you'll have on a ship."

"Umhum."

The large case was locked, and she locked a smaller one as Bobo appeared in the door. "Want a redcap, lady?" he asked. "Ten cents a bag."

"You may put them in the car, porter," she answered promptly, afraid she might break down and confess that she really didn't want to go to Europe at all.

Cinda was never loathe to pry into a person's affairs and try to set them in order; and while she had done a very nice job on the Daddy Fred situation, she couldn't fan Warren's lack of warmth into flame. So Paula found a quarter in her purse for

Bobo, and stood watching Cinda battle with him over it, scolding him and telling how greedy and rude he was, until he screamed for assistance.

"Run, Bobo!" she cried, holding Cinda's arms while he shoved the quarter into his shoe and grabbed the cases. "Put them in Lindsey's car."

"Honestly!" Cinda complained, shaking free and aiming a last kick at Bobo as he shot past her. "I should think he'd have more pride than to take money from a guest!"

"Yah-yah-yah," Bobo called back, banging his way down. "Who's a guest?"

Paula picked up her fur coat and a small hat made of velvet roses. "I'll call you and tell you what booking Daddy Fred makes for us," she said, looking about the room and wondering when she would see it again. "Aunt Maud will have the cottage, and we may be able to come for a little while, so don't look so glum."

"I feel glum," Cinda answered, wanting to pummel Warren the way she had shaken Bobo. "I suppose," she said, when they reached the landing with its stained glass window, "that it wouldn't do much good to make a wish—since you've decided to go."

"I'm afraid it wouldn't." Not all the stones in this window, or in the one below it, could change the summer. Five days of watching Warren had proved that to Paula. "I'll have such a lot to do in New York," she explained. "Daddy Fred said I can plan most of our itinerary, and we'll have to work it out with travel agencies."

Mrs. Hollister was in the library, so Paula ran in to say good-by to her. "Remember your promise to come up and have tea with Mother," she reminded, hugging her and hoping she wouldn't cry. "Any afternoon. And kiss Buff for me and—oh, I must tell Stella good-by."

If a few of her tears mingled with Stella's no one would notice it, for people always wiped off their cheeks after bidding Stella farewell. The very thought of riding on a train tore Stella apart; and she warned, "Now, you be careful, Paula. Sit in a middle coach—they're not apt to be so dangerous, if hit from in front or behind—and choose a seat in the middle of that. And don't talk to strangers."

"Oh, Lindsey is riding up with me." Paula dabbed at her face, and said with a laugh, "He insists that he likes to ride the commuter train. So he's going to deliver me to the hotel and come back this evening, with all the big businessmen. You know," she whispered loudly, "I think he has a date."

"No, he hasn't." Stella couldn't see Lindsey standing behind her, so she declared fiercely, "Not Lindsey. He's a steady, faithful boy, Lindsey is. If he likes a girl well enough to get on a train and take her all the way to New York, he won't go gallivantin' off the minute her back's turned. He don't like girls so much, anyway."

"I thank you." Lindsey answered against her ear, and made her jump. "Come on, Paula," he went on. "Don't believe old scared-cat, here. We'll miss the ten-fifty if we don't hurry, and I won't get home in time to make my red-head happy. Good-by, doll." He chucked Stella under her wrinkled chin, and hustled Paula into the front hall.

There were hurried kisses, with Cinda offering to drive to the station and bring Lindsey's car home, and Lindsey insisting he wanted the car left exactly where he intended to park it. And when Cinda had closed the door and followed her mother into the living room, she said unhappily, "It's pitiful, isn't it?"

"What is, dear?"

"The triangle: Jinx, Paula, War-Horse."

"Yes." Mrs. Hollister agreed, then turned to say with a bright smile, "but they're very young, thank goodness. They'll get over it."

"That's comforting." Cinda sat down on the arm of a chair, swinging her foot as she watched the car pull out into the street, and suggested, "It seems to me it's kind of like that thing you used to read us about the little elf man—'I'm as big for me, he said, as you are big for you.' Happiness hurts just as much when you're young as when you're older."

"I grant you that, honey; more, sometimes. But youth has more distractions. Lindsey will come home tonight and call up that cute, red-haired little Mitzi, and he'll go to the dance tomorrow night in a new dinner jacket, and next week he'll be back with his basketball. He won't have time to grieve over Paula. What is it he calls her?"

" 'A living doll.' "

"That's it. I never can keep up with him. He's always talking about 'dolls' or 'dogs,' and is either 'flipping,' or 'bailing out,' or 'rushing his motor' about something."

Cinda had to laugh at her mother's quoting Lindsey. It made him sound young and happy, and not too bruised inside. "I guess a trip to Europe will patch up Paula, too," she decided. "And having a few college men rushed in to sit around in night clubs with her will help. She likes that sort of thing. They won't be War-Horse, but . . . *Oh, help!*"

Mrs. Hollister watched her spring off the arm of the chair and duck back out of sight. "Who is it?" she asked.

"Page!" She pushed her mother into the center of the room, too, and cried, "Here he comes—and Jinx isn't here! Tell him I'm not at home or that I just dropped dead!"

"But, Cinda."

"Well, say I've just gone next door to the Masons'," Cinda thought up quickly, knowing how her mother hated to tell an untruth. "It'll surprise Mrs. Mason no end, but I won't have to stay long."

"Don't you want to see him?"

"No!" Cinda shook her head and ran for her coat. "He won't sit down like a human being," she said. "I've found that out. All he wants to do is ride around in that yellow peril of his, and I don't. It's cold, and the way he drives scares me stiff. He can't see beans with the top up, and he doesn't look even when it's down. I've had to ride with him a couple of times in the last few days, and—no, thank you. I'll pick my way to town on foot."

"Well, I'm glad." Mrs. Hollister watched Cinda speed for the kitchen, and called, "Don't forget to bring me some thread. And if you see Paul, I think you should tell him to come home and have a hot lunch."

"He can't," Cinda called back, winding her scarf about her head any old way. "Mr. Peterson gave him the afternoon off, so we're borrowing War-Horse's car and driving out to see his mother."

She forgot about Page as she came back to pick up a dropped glove and say, "Mrs. Banning's having tea for us, and she sounded all fluttery when she invited me. Would you like to go along?" she asked. "You used to know her."

"Perhaps next time, dear." Mrs. Hollister knew more about Mrs. Banning than Cinda thought she did. Accustomed to picking up remarks made by her children, here, there, and where she could, she had learned a great deal about Paul's mother; about his father, too. "I think it would be better," she said, as the doorbell rang, "for her to have today with Paul and you.

It will be the cozy kind of afternoon I have so often. Let her enjoy it."

"All right." Cinda stuffed her gloves into her pocket and made for the kitchen. "Tell that 'living boy-doll' on the porch," she shouted back, "that I've 'bailed out.' "

Chapter XII

The holidays were over. The Christmas tree stood propped against the back fence, far out by the alley. Its ornaments were piled, as usual, into their cartons, in Warren's empty closet, its string of lights lay in a tangle of dead wires on top of them.

Rainbows of bright dresses that had swept holiday parties the country over were hung away, too, and an army of sturdy shoes tramped the halls of high schools and colleges. Cinda, as one of the marchers, settled into the daily routine of meeting Kitty Lou on the corner five mornings each week, and adjusted to a busy, regimented day. Hot chocolate and sundaes in Peterson's, instead of in the little café across from school, had become the vogue; and every afternoon Mr. Peterson leaned on his counter and congratulated himself on the business his new young clerk had brought.

Groups of students pushed in and filled the booths. Cinda Hollister's crowd had started it; then, as word spread of an extra cherry and a larger dab of whipped cream, more and more had come, until the place was overflowing with youth. The old jukebox blared and its colored lights revolved as coins dropped into it; the magazines got a little roughed-up and the older folks complained, but Mr. Peterson sold lipsticks and pocket combs by the dozen and happily sent his charge customers a January statement that caused trouble in some homes.

Cinda was carrying a chocolate soda from the counter to a booth the day the new jukebox arrived. Paul hustled from behind the counter to unbolt and throw open the locked half of the double doors, and it rolled majestically in on a mover's dolly. It was the largest, most magnificent jukebox in town; and the movers strained and heaved to fit it in between the two counters where the old one had stood. Their work was hampered by the customers, who shrieked and dropped food while they offered advice.

In the midst of all the confusion, Cinda sidled over to Mr. Peterson. "What are you planning to do with the old one?" she asked.

"Turn it in."

"Would it cost very much to buy it?"

"I don't know." His thoughts were on the plate glass of his showcases, and he moved away, but she caught his sleeve.

"Could you ask that salesman over there?" she begged. "If it isn't too expensive, perhaps we could buy it for our big room at home. The men could deliver it right now."

"I'll see."

She saw Lindsey come in the door with his basketball teammates, and left her soda on a counter to push her way to him. "Jinx," she cried excitedly, "I think we can buy a jukebox! Wouldn't it be fun to have one, instead of an old record player? If we could put down all the cash we have, we could make payments on it."

"Not me." Lindsey went over to the fountain where Paul was on duty again, but Cinda pursued him.

"Now, you know you want it," she scolded. "You used to wish we had one."

"I'm going off to college next year," he answered equably.

"Why should I go in hock for something I can't use? You'll be going, too, in another year."

"Do you think Bobo and Buff would help pay? They'd have years and years of fun with it."

"Bobo? Hah! Buff? Double-hah! Bobo hasn't a nickel, and you know it; and Buff's too stingy to part with any of hers. How about letting me make myself a coke, Paul?"

"Help yourself."

Paul held out a glass, but Cinda crowded behind the counter, too. "I don't like to think we can't do something because we're getting too *old* to *want* to," she said reprovingly. "It doesn't seem right, at our age."

"Then why don't you buy yourself a doll and me a Davy Crocket cap?" Lindsey suggested, squirting syrup into a glass and adding charged water. "It makes as much sense as a jukebox, doesn't it, Paul?"

"Well . . ." Paul considered the matter. "I suppose you could go on enjoying a jukebox for a while longer," he said, taking a spoon from a holder and giving it to Lindsey. "You'll be around, off and on, for a few years, and you'll be coming home to visit. The little kids would like it, and your parents might get a boot out of dancing to it. But it would have made a better family gift if you'd bought it before Christmas."

"How right you are, how right you are!" Lindsey stirred his drink, satisfied his small savings account would remain intact.

But Cinda said with resignation, "All right. I guess I can give it up if I don't feel I'm too *old* to want it. I suppose I'd better go tell Mr. Peterson not to bother about asking the man how much it would cost."

She went away; and Lindsey shook his head. "Crazy, pure crazy," he said.

"I don't know about that." Paul wiped off the counter and said thoughtfully, "Cinda has something I wish I had—and she's holding on to it. When she's fifty, she'll still be young and a kid at heart. Look at her."

She was telling the jukebox good-by. They could see her stroking it, and could imagine her telling it, "Good-by, old pal. I hope someone will be kind to you."

"You'd think it was a broken down old race horse," Lindsey said, taking a swallow of his drink. "I wonder," he asked comfortably, "how much the darned thing would cost?"

He drifted to the back of the store; and when he and Cinda left, she pranced along beside him.

"I don't believe," she said excitedly, "that Moth and Daddy would think a hundred dollars would be too much, do you? If we all chip in?"

"The old thing goes bust about every other record," he mentioned glumly.

"But you only push a button in the back and it starts again. And who cares if the lights go off when they shouldn't? Oh, Jinx, just think of Buff and Bobo growing up to *loud* music!"

She was so pleased that the jukebox was to be allowed to spend the night in Mr. Peterson's prescription room, while the Hollisters considered its future, that she was in a fever to get home.

"I'd almost ride with Page," she laughed, chugging along beside Lindsey in the old sedan, "because he goes so fast. I'd *be* there by now. Why, do you know," she suddenly discovered, "he wasn't around this afternoon!"

"You shatter me. How did you bear it, not to have him breathing on you?"

"I managed," she retorted. "And, come to think of it, Kitty Lou didn't show up, either. Now, do you suppose . . . well, mercy me!"

She was off on another junket of thought. The jukebox was temporarily lost in what Lindsey called "the jungle of her mind," and he hoped it would stay there. But she found it again as soon as she entered the house.

The family received the proposition coldly. Bobo was the only one to shout, "Oh, boy!" because he had no money to invest. Buff threatened to move her hand-painted pig to a safer hiding place, and said with matter-of-fact good sense, "Bobo and I never get to dance at night. By the time we're old enough to, we'd have a worn-out jukebox. I'd rather wait and buy a better one, then."

"Yeah," Bobo echoed grandly. "We don't want a worn-out, old busted jukebox. We'll buy a brand new one when we're ready."

"And a car, and class rings," Mr. Hollister enumerated, ticking off expenses on his fingers, "and tickets to school entertainments, and dancing lessons, and autoharp lessons, and tennis lessons, and . . ."

"That's enough!" Cinda cried, to stop him. "I know I do get carried away with an idea—but I felt so sorry for the poor jukebox, being carted off and displaced by a beautiful new one. I always feel sorry for our cars when we turn them in," she defended sheepishly, "or when they end in a junk yard. Well, the bill before the senate has been voted on and defeated." The telephone rang, and she added, reaching back for it, "I know when I'm licked. Hello?"

"Oh, Cinda!" Kitty Lou's tearful voice answered. "I'm in such awful trouble. "Where's your father?" There was a gulping sob, followed by a wailing, "Oh, what will I *do*?" Then silence.

"What's happened? Kitty Lou? *Kitty Lou!*" Cinda begged bending over the mouthpiece, as if that would bring them closer together. "Where are you?"

"In a filling station out at the edge of town," a small, thin voice wept. "And the police are here, and—and the car's all smashed, and Page—Page says I did it. But I *didn't*. Oh, where's your father? He's Daddy's lawyer, isn't he?"

"Yes. Wait a minute." Cinda uncoiled the long extension and passed the telephone to Mr. Hollister in his easy chair. "Kitty Lou and Page have had some kind of an accident," she said, briefing him. "I can't understand much of what she says, so ask her if she's hurt."

The jukebox was forgotten as the Hollisters listened to him ask, "Are you hurt, child?"

"No—yes," Kitty Lou sobbed. "My—my forehead's hurt a little and—I can't walk very well, but that isn't the worst of it. Oh, I don't know what to *do!* A policeman wants to take me home, but Mother and Daddy aren't there. Could he bring me to your house?"

"Of course. Come as quickly as you can, and tell him I'll take care of the matter. Kitty Lou," he repeated sternly, so her frightened mind would accept the words, "get in the car and come. Don't wait to talk, just come. Shall I call Dr. Tuttle?"

"I—I guess so."

"Everything will be all right," he said, to calm her. "It's all right now. You're alive, and that's all that matters. I'll be out watching for you."

The connection was broken, as if someone at the other end had dropped the receiver and left it banging against a wall. He handed the telephone back to Cinda, and she said, listening vainly into it, "I knew something would happen with Page. I wonder what she meant when she said he blamed her for it?"

"We'll find out when she comes," her father answered. "You might get hold of Dr. Tuttle and ask him to stop by. Even if she isn't hurt, she'll be hysterical, and a sedative will help."

He got up and went to put on his overcoat, while Mrs. Hollister put her arm around a big-eyed, frightened Buff. "Run out and ask Stella to hold dinner," she said quietly. "Don't alarm her. Simply tell her some people are coming to see Daddy and that I'll be out to explain. Pretend you're acting a part in a play."

Cinda watched Buff go off and wished she had an errand to do. After an office nurse had taken the message for Dr. Tuttle, it was hard to sit and wait. It was still harder to stand behind the glass in the front door and watch a police car drive in, watch her father lean his hands on the open window and talk with the policeman inside. "I keep wondering," she said to Lindsey, who stood beside her, "what she meant by saying 'Page said I did it.' Did what?"

"We'll know in a minute."

Kitty Lou was being helped up the steps. She was holding a folded handkerchief to her eye; and when the policeman gave her a kind little pat before he went back to his car, she burst into tears.

"There, there, it's all right," Mr. Hollister soothed, getting her through the door Cinda held open. "You're safe with us, now, and nothing can happen to you. Not one thing worse than already has," he added. "Suppose you sit down and tell us about it."

"Oh, Cinda!" Kitty Lou crumpled up on Cinda's shoulder.

"I hate him!" she wept, her voice rising to a high, tremulous squeak. "I was so *scared*!"

Somehow, they got her coat off, got her into the living room and on the divan between Mrs. Hollister and Cinda. Lindsey saw her swollen right ankle and brought an ottoman from the library, then carefully slipped off her high-heeled pump, while Buff and Bobo kept at a staring distance.

It hurt when the shoe came off and her foot puffed more in release, but she only winced a little as she cried, "Oh, dear! I wish I'd never gone with him!"

"Let me see your eye, dear." Mrs. Hollister looked under the handkerchief at the swollen eye and skin abrasions, and sent Blair off to find the ice bag and put crushed ice in it. "This isn't so very bad," she said. And she asked, "Was Page hurt?"

"No! He wasn't even scratched. He wouldn't be!" Kitty Lou hid her face in her hands, and sobbed, "Oh, if I'd only minded my mother!"

It seemed as if she might go on sobbing indefinitely, so Cinda, who knew her best, stopped patting her shoulder and said crossly, "Kitty Lou, we're not going to learn anything, or know what to do, if you don't sit up and tell us what happened. Did your mother tell you not to go with Page?"

"No." Kitty Lou dabbed at her eyes and stared fixedly at the patent leather pump Lindsey still held. "I went home from school," she managed to mumble, "because I'd promised to help Mother take some stuff to the rummage sale at the church. And while we were loading, the car, Daddy telephoned and said he had to go to East Orange and see about his other store." She began to slump again, but Cinda propped her up, and she went on, "He wanted Mother to pick him up right away and go with him, and Mother got all excited, so I promised I'd stay with you until she came back. And if you had company, she said I was to eat in the Bon Ton Tea Room. Oh, I meant to," she wailed. She cast another miserable glance at the pump, and sobbed, "I—I carried the baskets back in and got dressed up—but I meant to."

"So you meant to." Cinda had been aware of the high heels and plaid wool dress, and she looked from her own brown brogues to her father who was pulling a chair across to the divan, and remarked pointedly, "We always put on our best clothes for dinner."

"I know it was silly." Kitty Lou stopped to think about the yellow car that had come charging along the street as she tripped up to Peterson's Pharmacy and Luncheonette, exactly as she had hoped it would. Page never arrived until he could make an entrance. "Well," she said hesitantly, "Page drove up, and I stopped, and—and we went for a ride. But I guess you know that."

From there on the story became so jumbled that it took endless prodding to get any of it straight. The Hollisters managed to follow the yellow car out of town and onto a two-lane, well-traveled road before Kitty Lou broke down again. "Ohhhh!" she groaned with a shudder. "If I had to live through that again I'd die. I'd just die, that's all. But I didn't touch the wheel, I didn't!"

"Kitty Lou." Mr. Hollister took his turn at drawing out the story. "This is the part we have to know about," he said patiently. "What caused the accident, how fast you were going, everything you can tell us."

"All right." She took the ice bag Bobo handed her and swiped at her tears with the soiled handkerchief. "I guess I can tell you about it," she said, swallowing and trying to take a deep breath. "We started out about like anyone would, except that it was awfully cold, and I wished the top was up. But I didn't mind too much. And then—suddenly—when we first got on the narrow road, Page yelled, 'Do you want to see something funny?' And without thinking, I yelled back, 'Sure.'

"A car was coming toward us." She stared straight ahead as if seeing the approaching car again, her fists clenched, her face strained and her breathing heavy, before she said, "It was almost dark by then. The car's lights were on, so Page turned his on, too. And he moved right over onto the wrong side of the road. And the other car kept coming, and coming, and coming, with its horn blowing. And then—just before it reached us—it pulled clear off on the graveled shoulder, and went bumping along with two of its wheels almost down in the ditch. There was a woman in it, with a lot of little children—I saw her as she went by. And Page leaned out and yelled, 'Chicken!' at her."

Mr. Hollister glanced quickly at his wife, then up at Lindsey, and shook his head.

Kitty Lou was sobbing again, but she said as best she could, "Page did it twice more, and all the time I was begging him not to. He just laughed and kept yelling 'chicken' at people. And then—then one car didn't turn out quickly enough, or didn't seem to know which way to go, and . . . " She swallowed again, but went on, "Page jerked his wheel so fast that we sideswiped a cement bridge, and the fender smashed and a tire blew out. Page couldn't keep us straight or stop fast enough, and I saw a big *thing* flying at us."

"What sort of a 'thing,' dear?" Mrs. Hollister asked gently.

"An underpass, I guess you call it. It was made of stone; and I was pushing down on the floor so hard, just as if I could stop the car when I hadn't any brake, that—when we hit it, I suppose I sprained my ankle. We weren't going so very fast by then," she explained, "just kind of bouncing and weaving along; and when we smacked into the stone wall, my forehead banged into something. The whole front of the car was smashed in and we were half on the road and half off."

"Did anyone stop to help you?" Lindsey asked.

"Oh, yes," she looked up to say. "A man came through the underpass, right that second. He coasted along a little way, so he could stop on the shoulder, and just as he was coming back to us, a patrol car came under, too, and the cop saw us.

"He . . . " Her blue eyes were enormous and very honest as she looked straight at Mr. Hollister to say, "After he found we were all right, the patrol cop asked us what had happened, and Page said his tire had blown out. He said the other car was coming through the underpass—the one with the man in it—and that I'd got scared of meeting it there, and grabbed the wheel. He said he could have kept the car straight if I hadn't grabbed the wheel. He kept saying it, over and over."

"I see." Mr. Hollister leaned forward and took her hand in his. "Kitty Lou," he said, "that was a bad experience for you. We know you're telling us a straight story, so let me ask you one or two more questions."

"But will he sue me?" Kitty Lou dropped the ice bag to clutch him and beg, "You won't let him sue me, will you? He said his father's going to. He said I'd ruined a three thousand dollar car, and as soon as he gets it towed away, he's going to tell his father and make Daddy buy him a new one, or sue us."

"He won't sue you, Kitty Lou, I promise you that. Listen to me, child." He held her twitching hands, and said, smiling at her, "I'll have a talk with Page's father. I imagine he'll be very happy if you don't sue *him*. The thing for you to do, now, is to let Cinda bring you in some dinner. You two girls can have it quietly together, and when your parents come for you, we'll go into the story again. Can you do that?"

"I think so." Her smile quivered in answer to his and she

put the ice bag back on her forehead, but she sighed, "I do hate to tell Mother and Daddy."

"You needn't, darling." Mrs. Hollister bent over to kiss the cleanest spot on her cheek, and to comfort, "They'll be frightened, of course, because of what might have happened, but they'll be thankful, too, because you're safe. And now, let's not talk about it any more, for a while."

Bobo followed her out to the dining room, and offered, scowling, "He sure is a louse, isn't he?"

"Yes," she answered, separating the new television tables and setting up two. "Something's very wrong with a boy who deliberately jeopardizes the lives of other people, to say nothing of his own, and who consciously blames someone else. He's either very weak and afraid, or needs more discipline."

"He's a rotten, dishonest louse." Bobo had expressed his opinion, so he went on to feed Down Boy; and his father took his place.

"It's unbelievable," Mr. Hollister said, "this business of making cars take to the side of the road. I asked Kitty Lou if she had told the patrol cop about it, and she said she's tried to, but that Page did all the talking; and the cop, once he'd learned their names, was only interested in getting the car off the road."

"But the policeman who brought her here?" Mrs. Hollister asked. "Who was he, and where did he come from? Didn't she talk to him?"

"Not much, which is just as well. He answered the radio call and took her to the service station, where she telephoned us. You see, honey," he pointed out, "there isn't any way to prove that she *didn't* grab the wheel, or that Page crowded those people off the road. It's her word against his. I wish I could find any one of them."

"Do you think you can, Don?"

"I'll certainly give it a try. It's a hundred to one shot," he answered thoughtfully, his mind already on tomorrow. "The newspapers won't play up the accident because no one was hurt. It was just a little mishap that often occurs on the road. A little mishap! The rich boy's unfortunate smashup. If a reporter goes out to the Vandergren's to ask about it, he'll come away with an ear-to-ear grin and his pocket full of cigars. Gosh, Fran," he said, "to give that boy a car is like giving a kid a loaded gun and telling him to go out and play with it, but to be sure and shoot himself, not someone else." Muscles tightened along his jaws as he said, "A lot of people are exposed to Page on the highways: our kids are, we are, our friends, people we've never heard of."

"I know." The doorbell rang, and she said, "That's Dr. Tuttle, darling. I'll let him in, then stay with Kitty Lou while he examines her, if you'll remove Buff from that chair she's glued to, and send her out to help Stella."

"I'll shoo her out." He put his arm around her waist, and murmured with his cheek against her hair, "Oh, Fran, I wish all our kids were little again."

Chapter XIII

CINDA walked to school alone the next morning.

Dr. Tuttle had suggested, since today was Friday, that Kitty Lou skip classes for one day and be kept quiet over the week end. "You'd scare the boys with that black eye," he had teased. And with the sedative taking effect, her southern accent had returned and she had drawled, "I suah don't want anybody to see me lookin' this way, especially that horrible ol' Page Vandergren."

But Page was not at school, either. The entrance hall buzzed with conversation, its whispered excitement almost as great as on the morning Mary Spillman had eloped. Word of the accident had spread. A voluble fat girl's father was the patrolman who had arrived just after the crash; and as Cinda pushed her way up the steps, she was telling all who stopped to listen, "And she grabbed the wheel. I don't see why she'd want to do that with *Page* driving! He's such a *marvelous* driver!"

"She didn't grab the wheel!" Cinda answered her, loud enough for the whole group to hear.

Then she stopped, because her father had warned her at breakfast, "Don't talk about it, honey. I know it's hard not to defend or deny, but it's useless. Barbie and Marty will have to know, I suppose, but until I get in touch with Mr. Vandergren, let's keep it quiet."

So she had clamped her lips shut and walked on to her locker. She saw heads turn to watch her, but she hung away her coat and went on to the ramp. Paul was leaning against the wall, waiting for her.

He laid her books on top of his, and said, as they walked up together, "Page went to New York this morning."

"He did?"

It seemed right for Paul to know about the accident. He had stopped by on his way home from work to leave a book for Lindsey, and had met the Chappells helping Kitty Lou out to their car. And Lindsey had sat on the arm of the divan and told him the truth.

"I saw him getting on the train with his father," he said in a low tone, not to be overheard by more eager students who passed them. "They looked chatty enough."

"I wonder where they were going?" Cinda mused. "And where the whole family was last night when Mr. Chappell kept calling. Anyone would think that common decency would make them call up to ask how Kitty Lou is."

"Page probably said she wasn't hurt. You don't know what he said, Cinda."

"No." Cinda stopped before the door to her home room, and said thoughtfully, "Somehow, it doesn't seem like Page. I knew he was thoughtless and selfish, and terribly, terribly spoiled, but I can't picture him as a liar and a skunk. It doesn't fit with the kind of kids we know. And that crazy driving!"

"He does it for a thrill," Paul told her. "Some guys like to spin their cars. They take them over on the race track and get them going at a good speed, then throw them into a skid and spin around. It's quite a sport."

"But at least they aren't risking the lives of other people, just their own. That's the awful thing, Paul—chasing people off the road, then laughing at them. Well, he can't do it for a while, not without a car."

She took her books from the pile he held on his arm, as he said jubilantly, "Gosh, I almost forgot! This is my night off, and the Thompsons aren't going out. I won't have to baby-sit, so how about going to the basketball game?"

"And how about coming to our house for dinner first?" she accepted. "We'll have an early dinner because Moth and Daddy always have to go and root for Jinx. Daddy," she laughed, "growls at the referee whenever he calls a foul on our team, and Moth covers her eyes every time Jinx gets spilled. She sees most of the game from between her fingers, and Daddy's practically apoplectic, but they have a whale of a time. Six o'clock?"

"Thanks. See you then."

She worked her way through a busy day, and after an hour with Kitty Lou, who was languid in new Christmas lounging pajamas, hurried home to set the table for Stella.

Only a few weeks before, she would have walked along, watching for a low-slung yellow car, not daring to dream of ever riding in it, just hoping to see it cruise along the street, its motor purring in quiet satisfaction, but ready to give a deep, warning growl that could turn into a roar.

There was no yellow car, now; and she walked the two blocks home, thinking how many changes the Christmas holidays had brought.

Paula's polite little letter of thanks for her visit hadn't sounded like Paula. Lindsey had gone to the New Year's dance alone and had left early; Melody Ayer had gone with Dick.

Paul's mother—and she liked that change—had sneaked out his father's tuxedo and dared drive in town with it, all alone, so she could see where Paul lived and where he worked. . . . And now this.

Golly, she thought, walking along, it's bound to wreck the gang. Everybody's going to take sides, and Kitty Lou won't come to parties if Page does. I don't want him around, either, and I'm not as good at hiding my feelings as Jinx is. I'm apt to blow a gasket when I see him. Thank goodness, I won't have to meet him until Monday, anyway.

She had a good week end. Glenvale high school defeated its bitterest rival, and a large number of students celebrated the victory in Mr. Peterson's store. It was shouting bedlam, with Mr. Peterson unable to fill orders fast enough, spilling, breaking glasses and dropping spoons, while he coaxed for quiet and more time. So, even though it was Friday night, Paul gave up his freedom and took over. And Lindsey joined him in a comedy team behind the soda fountain, white caps on the side of their heads.

"There you are, my good man," Lindsey would say, pushing a drink across the counter with a flourish. "Wait a minute, you forgot to pay papa." And he would hover above the open cash register, gruesomely kneading his fingers over the beautiful quarters and dimes.

Paul was quicker and more adept. He flipped ice cream into a glass, added a dash of charged water, a splatter of whipped cream, stirred, and passed the drink across, all in time to a tune he whistled.

"Step right up, folks," Lindsey kept shouting, "step right up. Place your orders. Or give them to the little lady," he would add, meaning Cinda, who was trying to help poor Mr. Peterson, too.

It was fun; it was different; it was a good Friday night. Saturday and Sunday were good, too, except when the doorbell rang, Cinda peeked out uncertainly, fearful it might be Page. And on Monday, she literally dragged Kitty Lou to school.

"I don't want to sit in the same room with him," Kitty Lou kept repeating like a mournful lament. "I nevah knew anyone I couldn't speak to befoah. And I don't know how to act, cooped up in theah with him, an' not bein' able to look at him. Is my eye awful?"

"The bruise hardly shows," Cinda answered truthfully, but privately thinking that Kitty Lou would have aroused more sympathy had she borne some scars. "That make-up your mother put on really covers it. Now act as if nothing had happened."

"I can't. I reckon Page has been tellin' everybody how awful I am. And if your father won't let me tell my side of the story . . ."

"He will, Kitty Lou. Daddy simply said," Cinda explained, as had her father before her, "we'll keep 'officially' still. The longer Mr. Vandergren waits to get in touch with you, the worse it looks for him. You were a passenger in his son's car, and you were hurt. Daddy talked to him about that, yesterday—not as a lawyer, but as one of the few people Mr. Vandergren used to like in this town. Now he doesn't like Daddy much, and he doesn't believe that Page crowds people off the road. You can say what you like, but Page said it first and louder, and there just isn't any proof, either way. You say Page drove on the wrong side of the road 'til he got bluffed out, he says you jerked the wheel. Who's going to know which one is telling the truth?"

"I am."

"I know it." Kitty Lou had stopped again, so Cinda gave her another tug. "Your real friends know it, too," she said, "so why not let Daddy handle it? He's an attorney. And he wants to see Page grounded for the sake of other people's safety. Talking about it isn't going to do any good—and nobody's going to remember much about it after a week end, anyway."

"All right." Kitty Lou gave a vast sigh and capitulated. "I won't talk about it unless I'm asked to," she said, "but if I am, I'll tell the truth—no matter if I'm believed, or not." She stopped again, and no amount of tugging could budge her. "*Ohhh!*" she cried, shaking Cinda off to point. "*Look!* Look there!"

A long red car was sliding into the parking spot a yellow one had always occupied. It was as long and red as a fire chief's, and hugged the ground like a dragon.

"So *that's* why they went to New York," Cinda said, stopping to stare, too.

"I'm going home."

"You are not." An admiring crowd had gathered around the car; and Cinda took Kitty Lou firmly by the arm. "We're going right in that school and toss our heads!" she cried, mad all the way through. "Our whole gang's going to look right past Mr. Page Vandergren, and not see him. Maybe that will show people what we think of him."

"Page won't care." Kitty Lou's lips began to tremble. "He has a new car and I'm all banged-up. I don't want to go to school," she said in a quivering voice.

"I don't blame you, but you have to. Listen," Cinda pointed

out practically, "if you stay home today, you'll want to stay home tomorrow. Coming back will be even harder to do."

"But my ankle—I can't walk very well."

"You're walking all right. Buck up, here we go."

They swept up the walk with Kitty Lou trying not to limp at such a fast pace, swept up the inside steps and to their lockers. "Hurry," Cinda whispered, hoping they could get upstairs and into their seats before Page came jauntily in with his followers. "I'll go home to lunch today, instead of eating in the cafeteria, so I can tell Daddy about Page's new car."

But her father didn't come home to lunch; and Kitty Lou didn't go back to school.

"Mothah says I don't have to," she told Cinda over the telephone. "She says I'm too nervous to go. Did you see the way Page actually *grinned* at me this mornin'? He looked right straight at me, and *grinned.*"

"I saw it. He tried to grin at me, too. Well, I'll stop by and report," Cinda promised, before she hung up.

It was a long afternoon. She decided not to go to Peterson's because Page was sure to be parked in front. Nothing would be the same: not the jukebox or chatting over the counter with Paul. Page would swagger in and try to squeeze into whatever booth she occupied with Barbie and Marty, and the whole afternoon would be unhappy. The good old times, it seemed, were gone forever.

She left Kitty Lou's and parted regretfully from Barbie, who said with a shrug, "You're being foolish. Why should we stop liking Page just because he banged Kitty Lou up? He's going to be around—very much around, with that new Jaguar—so why should we stay home and let him have all the fun?"

It was sensible advice, in its way. Why, indeed? I suppose,

Cinda thought, walking on alone, that if everyone stayed away from everyone he didn't admire, the theaters, restaurants, even the streets, would be awfully empty. She almost turned around, but she couldn't.

I might have been the one who was riding with him, she went on telling herself, if I hadn't found out how reckless he is and hadn't got tired of the demanding way he treated me. I can't go walking into Peterson's and act as if nothing's happened. About the first time he hung over my table and twinkled at me, I'd "flip my lid," as Jinx says. I hope Jinx won't give him the glad hand of friendship.

Lindsey came roaring in at five-thirty, his short hair still damp from a shower after practice, his jacket slung over his shoulder. "Say," he called, seeing Cinda in the library, lonely and bored stiff with a magazine, "did you see the wagon that joker's got?"

"How could I miss it?" She gave her magazine a toss, and invited, "Come in and start sneezing. Stella says you'll 'catch' pneumonia if you don't wait to get dry and put on your coat. Is it really a Jaguar?"

"From bumper to bumper. Poor old Minnie almost dropped her headlights when it pulled out ahead of her. The old girl wheezed to keep up, but she couldn't make it. Oh, well, the filthy rich have all the luck. I'm bushed."

He stretched out on the long divan; and Cinda got up to turn on more lamps. She could hear her mother coming down the stairway with Buff; and Buff's high, sweet little voice saying, "The dance recital's to be next Friday, and it doesn't seem quite fair for Charmion's mother to buy her a new dress for it, does it?"

"Not unless," Lindsey mumbled, "she buys her a new set of teeth to go with it. Straight ones."

"It's so soon after Christmas," Buff trilled wistfully on. "A new dress would be lovely, though, don't you think? So stimbalating."

"Stim-u-lating," Lindsey mumbled again, more drowsily this time, as his mother answered,

"We'll look over your wardrobe, darling. I think your pink nylon with the lace would be lovely, but we'll see. Help me turn on the lamps, so we'll have the living room bright and gay for Daddy."

She went about flipping switches and adjusting shades, while Buff assured the occupants of the two rooms that, no matter how old her dress might be, she would dance so lightly and with such grace that the new, expensive frocks on her competitors would never be noticed.

"Shy and ragged, that's our Buff," Lindsey mumbled for the third time; and gave up trying to snatch a nap.

Mr. Hollister came in exactly on time, but so quietly that his wife, starting for the door and his evening welcome, hesitated, her face puzzled. No "by all the gods" announced him, neither to preface the fact that Lindsey's car was in the driveway nor where it belonged, and he tossed his hat and coat on the fireside bench, instead of hanging them neatly away, as was his custom.

"I want to have a little talk with all of you," he said, absently returning his wife's kiss and leading her into the library. "Is Bobo around?"

"He's feeding Down Boy, I guess," Lindsey answered, "and heckling Stella. Want me to bring him in?"

"If you will, son." Mr. Hollister dropped into his chair and fumbled in his pocket for a cigarette. "Thanks, baby," he said, as Buff sprang to light it for him.

"Oh, you're welcome, Dadda." She perched on the arm of his chair, one arm around his neck, and asked pleasantly, "Are you going to scold us, Dadda?"

"No, darling." He reached out for his wife's hand; and as she sat down on the ottoman before him, he said gently, "I think I'll go a little soft and tell you all how much you mean to me."

He watched Bobo follow Lindsey in, licking chocolate icing from his upper lip, and went on, "Sit down, boys, this won't take too long. I have something to tell you, and perhaps a little speech to make. I just came from the Chappell's."

"Oh, Daddy, has Page been to see them?" Cinda, unable to wait, slid out on the edge of her chair; but he shook his head.

"Page," he said carefully, "won't be driving for at least a year. He's had his license revoked."

Some gave exclamations of pleasure, some expressed amazement, but his whole audience sat up.

"I didn't know how I was going to do it," he admitted, tapping his cigarette against an ashtray, "but I knew it had to be done. That boy can't be allowed on the road. So I tried talking to his father first, and got nowhere. He didn't believe me. But with the car laid up, I figured I'd have plenty of time. Then I heard about the new one, and—well, I got busy."

"How, Daddy?" Cinda asked. "What did you do?" The suspense was so great that she shoved her mother over and sat on half of the big ottoman.

"It turned out to be fairly simple. Kitty Lou thought the car the woman was driving was either light tan or gray; she was almost sure it was. And I decided that a woman who had a bunch of children with her might very easily live around in that neighborhood. I thought I'd ask the state police to keep an eye out for her, and the local, too. But I didn't think I'd have such luck."

"What luck, Dad?" Lindsey asked.

"Pure, unadulterated good fortune." The cigarette had burned down, and, putting it out in his ashtray, Mr. Hollister said with a pleased grin, "I went down to talk it over with a police captain I know. And, bless me, if the woman hadn't already called in and reported the whole business! The desk sergeant showed me a memo on it."

"Then why hadn't they done something about it?" Lindsey demanded. "Kitty Lou tried to tell a cop. Why didn't they put two and two together, and do something?"

"I don't know." His father sighed and shook his head, "Perhaps," he said, "because the woman called the local station instead of the state police. She does live in town, and had gone out after eggs. Or perhaps because she couldn't describe the car too well. She said the lights blinded her and she was trying to keep out of the ditch; so all she knew was that 'it was an open car and looked kind of foreign.' The police can't investigate every call they get about bad drivers or road hogs when it's too late to catch them, so they just take down the information and file it, in case they need it later."

"They sure needed this one," Bobo breathed, as round-eyed as if he were at the movies. He could see a fleeing red car, police giving chase, shots, the villain surrendering with his hands up; and he asked, "Is Page in jail?"

"No." His father hated to ruin the climax for him, but he said, "The Captain and I went to talk with the woman, then we talked with Kitty Lou's father, and Mr. Vandergren came out from New York and brought Page down to headquarters. The ending isn't as dramatic as you'd like it to be, but it's very satisfactory. Page will have his license suspended. His father says, by the way, that he'll be sent off to school."

"Good!" Cinda clapped her hands and almost fell off the stool as she cried, "He would run away! I suppose he couldn't ride the school bus or walk like the rest of us do, and couldn't face us."

"Wait a minute, honey," Mr. Hollister said. "That's the thing I want to talk to you about, the thing that makes Page what he is. I met his mother. She came up to wait for her husband in my office, and she's a nice little woman. She told me that they have an older daughter, happily married, and a son who was graduated from MIT and has a good engineering job. It seems her husband came up the hard way, and it was tough sledding when the older kids were small. His money didn't start rolling in until Page was growing up, and he took a notion that the boy must have everything he'd missed in life. So you see," he said thoughtfully, "he gave it to him. Everything but the important things—love and security. And that brings on my speech."

"We aren't rich people," he said, leaning forward and letting his eyes travel lovingly over the group, "but we want to give you good things, too. There isn't a day, or an hour, or a minute, when you aren't on our minds, your mother's or mine. But the things we want to give you aren't the luxuries Page got. We want you happy, and we want you secure."

"We are, Daddy," Cinda said.

He seemed not to hear her, for he went on, grinning a little and looking off into space, "I covered a lot of years as I drove home tonight. I went clear back to when you were little, and I used to think it was darned hard going. Each one of you took a turn at telling lies in spite of me—and telling on each other. And when we took a trip in the car, we stopped more than we went. And you always needed something, shoes, clothes, or fillings in your teeth. And there was always one of you sure to be sick in bed, if your mother and I wanted to go somewhere. And yet I rode along and wished I had that time back again."

His wife leaned over and smiled at him. "I know what you were thinking, Don," she said softly. "Your mother said it to me, once, when Buff was screaming for her bottle, and Bobo had fallen downstairs, and Cinda had taken off to some child's house without asking, and the older boys were quarreling over a baseball mitt. I wanted to clap on my hat and run; and your mother said, 'Enjoy these years while you can, Frances; they're very short. This is the time when you're all here together. When you light the lamps in the evening, the children are all here at home; and when you lock the doors at night, they're all safe in their beds.' I've never forgotten that."

"And now we know she was right. We can't keep you here with us forever, and we can't follow you when you're away. We wouldn't if we could. I guess," Mr. Hollister said, "we're like a couple of parent birds. We have to push you out of the nest and teach you to fly. Just little flights, at first; just awkward little flights that bump along the ground and hurt us as much as you. You have to try your wings, but remember this: the nest is always here, and a few crash landings aren't going to keep you from finding happiness and reaching whatever goal you set out for—if you fly in the right direction."

Cinda glanced across at Lindsey. He was sitting hunched forward, listening intently to his father. And while she wondered what was passing through his mind, he said, "Thanks,

Dad. When the going gets rough, I bet I'll remember that little speech."

And Buff leaned down to entreat, "Please, Dadda, talk some more. I want to write it in my diary, so that when I'm grown-up, I can read to my children, 'How well I remember the night my father talked to us.' "

"There isn't any more to say, baby," he answered, surprised to have said so much. "Don't you know that if people talk too long, scold too long, entertain too long, or address a jury too long, ears close up? I'm an attorney, and I learned that early. Now is the time to stop."

"That's the way I'm going to do it," Bobo volunteered, thinking of the icing Stella might have thrown out by now. "When I'm a lawyer, I'm going to make my speeches short and snappy. 'Those are the facts,' I'll say to the jury. 'It's up to you to find my client not guilty.' And if I decide to be a prosecuting attorney, I'll just turn it around and ask to have him electrocuted. Can I go, now?"

"If you like." Mr. Hollister looked down at Cinda, who was leaning on his knees, looking up at him. "Have you a question, ma'am?" he asked.

But she only shook her head and smiled at him. "I had a dozen a little while ago," she said. "But now I'm only thinking how wise you were when you told us not to talk about Page and stir up a lot of useless fuss and arguments. I couldn't accept his being in the crowd again, for what he did to Kitty Lou and the things he said; and I'm afraid I thought more about that than about how dangerous he was to himself and other people. And now I'm feeling sorry for him. Do you suppose," she asked, her upturned eyes earnest, "that I'm going to be the kind of bird that doesn't ever learn to fly? A chicken or a duck, maybe, that just kind of pecks around and doesn't get anywhere?"

"My dear little friend." Her father cupped her chin in his hand, and answered, as sincere and sober as she, "You're a loyal little bird. And if trying will get you off the ground, you're going to turn out to be one of our very best flyers."

Cinda turned her face so that her cheek lay in the caressing hollow of his palm. "Thank you, Daddy," she said softly. "No matter if I fly to the ends of the earth, I'll always fly back home again."

Chapter XIV

ON SATURDAY morning, Cinda leaned against the newel post on the top landing and considered the beautiful window in front of her. "I suppose I ought to stop making wishes," she told herself, going over to the padded seat and kneeling on it, her arms crossed on the oak sill. "It's such a childish thing to do that I'd be ashamed to let even Buff see me. I guess I'll stop."

The colors were so soft and beautiful. She let her hand pass back and forth over them, traced the leaded outline of a leaf, a stem, a pinkly glowing rose, and let her finger rest on a ruby that held flower and stem together. "It's just a silly window," she said, keeping her finger there. "It shuts out the view of trees and the street, and makes us put a light on long before it's really dark. And, anyway, I haven't any special wish to make, so early in the day."

She heard Lindsey come out of his room and tramp along the hall. "Good grief, are you still around?" he asked at the top of the stairs. Then he went on down, and remarked over his shoulder, "You look like a praying mantis. I thought Mom wanted you to go to town."

"She does. I've been waiting for the list." I hope he gets a letter from Paula, she wished silently and quickly, having to hustle with something before she let go of the stone.

Then she began to laugh. The morning mail was already on the hall table and Lindsey was leafing through the bills and circulars. A letter from Paula would either be there or it wouldn't, and no wish on a ruby could change it, now. I shouldn't have been in such a rush, she thought ruefully, forgetting she had decided to give up her childish game. Something really important might come up today. It usually does.

"Well, what do you know!" Lindsey held up a white, square envelope and squinted speculatively at it. "Well, blow me down."

"Is it from Paula?" she asked eagerly, leaning forward to look through the spindles in the banister.

"Nope. It's from a fraternity at Michigan State."

He turned the letter over to look at the return address, and was so disgustingly slow about slitting the flap, that she got up and hung over the railing behind him. "Don't you ever read your mail?" she asked, out of patience with him.

"Sometimes–in privacy."

He crushed the letter into his hip pocket and looked up to smirk at her; and she saw the other letter before he did.

"There's one from Paula," she said, pointing, recognizing the handwriting.

"Oh, from the kid." That one disappeared into his pocket, too, without so much as a rapturous glance at it, or a caress for the paper Paula's pen had touched. "Mr. Lindsey P. Hollister is having himself quite a day," he remarked. "I'll pick you up at the market." And off he went to the kitchen.

"Well!" She had wasted a perfectly good wish on Lindsey. And since she rarely received a letter, there was no reason to sort the mail again. Nothing remained but a dull tour of a supermarket.

She got her coat and scarf from the closet, and was just going down the porch steps when she saw Page cross the street and come toward the driveway. On foot. Walking.

She hadn't seen him since that one day in school, and couldn't remember ever having seen him in his leather coat, with his feet taking turns at touching the ground for any great distance. Her first impulse was to run back inside, then she walked on to meet him, and said a cool, "Hello." And from long habit, she added, "Jinx is eating breakfast."

"Thanks. Were you going somewhere?"

"Just—just to town," she stuttered.

"Mind if I walk along?"

"Why, no." He sounded so humble that she let him fall into step beside her.

"I suppose you've heard that I'm going off to school," he said uncomfortably, watching her nod. "I had it coming to me, but I don't want to go. I'd rather stick around and get another chance, but my dad can't see it that way. He says I've disgraced the family, and I suppose I have. He says this will make a man of me."

"Do you think it will?" she found herself asking.

"I don't know." He kicked a stick off the sidewalk, and said without much certainty, "I'm no good, but I can give it a try."

"You *are* good, Page!" she cried. "Everybody's good, if he'll let himself be. We all do things that are wrong. What you did just happened to be *awfully* wrong, and dangerous to other people, and—and not very honest."

She had to say that much, had to let him know she couldn't condone his mistakes, but she added, to let him know she forgave them, "Nobody's going to keep on holding it against you."

"My father won't believe that. He's so ashamed that he's kept me in hiding all week. He wants to ship me out as fast as he can, but—well, I didn't want to go away without telling you good-by, Cinda. I'm an awful crumb, and I'll probably stay one, but I wanted to tell you good-by."

He stopped and held out a hesitant hand, but she put her left mitten into it instead of her right, and kept on walking. "You're going to buy me a coke," she said, as, coupled to her, he had to move along, too. "Right in the drugstore. And you're going to tell Paul good-by, and Jinx, when he comes along to pick up my groceries, and anyone else who comes in. You're not going to sneak away as if you're afraid to see us."

"I am, though," he protested. "You're the only one I felt as if I really had to see. I didn't want you to hate me."

"Pooh!" she laughed. "I hated you like crazy for a couple of days—and I think it was natural for me to—but I don't, anymore. Kitty Lou won't, later."

"Don't mention her!" For a moment he looked like the old arrogant Page, then he shook his head and said frankly, "I planned to apologize to her, but my father queered it. He offered Mr. Chappell a thousand dollars for what I'd done to Kitty Lou, but Mr. Chappell thought it was a bribe so I could keep my license—and heaved him out. I don't blame him, but—gosh, I couldn't get within a block of the Chappells'."

"Well, perhaps you can write her a letter sometime, and, of course, I'll tell her." They had reached the drugstore; and as he hung back, she cried, "Oh, stop acting so silly! Not over fifty people in this whole town know you can't go swooping along Main Street any more, and they don't care. You're the one who cares. Buck up!"

She marched him inside and made an airy sign to Paul. And

if Paul's eyes widened, his slow grin spread immediately afterward, and he said naturally, "Hi. What'll it be?"

Page was awkward at first. He sat in a booth, close to the wall, and only nodded at a few people he knew. He was a whipped, hangdog Page that made Cinda wonder what he had endured during the week. And he defiantly smoked one cigarette after another.

"Look, chum, you're imitating a chimney," Cinda said, when her coke was gone and half her morning with it. "It's all very nice for me to do my Girl Scout deed of the day, but I have groceries to buy. If I don't have any bags of groceries, Jinx will be wild."

The door banged open in the way Lindsey always opened a door, so hard it hit the magazine rack, just as it always whacked the radiator at home, and she peeked around the side of the booth.

"So *there* you are!" Lindsey shouted, charging toward her. "I double park, then go around the block, and double park and go around again, and here you sit." Then he saw Page and stopped, just before he murdered one sister. His jaw dropped, he couldn't control that, but his voice held its crossness as he went on scolding, "What do you mean by leading a housewife astray? How do you think we're going to eat at our house if she sits here, talking to you?"

"I don't know," Page answered.

"It's time you found out. You," Lindsey said, stabbing his finger at Page's chest, the way he always did when arguing with the referee before he was thrown out of a basketball game for five personal fouls, "will have to come and help me buy the groceries. We can't trust her."

"Thanks." Page looked up with a grateful grin. Having Lindsey stand by was as good as poling a large majority vote. It meant much the same as an old slogan which says, "As Maine goes, so goes the nation." Lindsey was power. He was the whole Glenvale High. He was the guy who, in the next four years, would put Glenvale on the athletic map. If he chose to accept Page Vandergren as a decent citizen, others would, too.

"Come on," Lindsey said, snapping his fingers for the list. "Let this silly girl sit here in a booth. We have men's work to do."

Page slid along the seat. "Cinda," he said, pressing his hands flat on the formica table top, "You Hollisters don't know what you've done for me. Even I don't, yet. I may grow up hating your father, or I may wish I had one like him. It all depends on how straight I can keep my thinking after I get away from here. But," he hesitated, then said, "I'd like to write to you, sometimes. Can I?"

"Oh, please do." Cinda reached across and covered his hands with hers. "I was feeling sad, just this morning, because I never get any letters," she said. "And I wasted a wish for Jinx to get one. Now I'll wish for myself. Good luck, Page."

"Thanks again."

He went out with Lindsey's broad hand slapping his back; and Paul slid into his place. "How did it happen?" Paul asked without preamble.

"He came to tell me good-by," Cinda answered, "for some strange reason."

She looked across at Paul, resting on his elbow, his thin face happy in repose, his white cap jaunty on his light hair; and she compared his life to Page's. Paul had a father who had squandered his money on himself, and now wanted his son to work for him and cost him nothing. Page's father wanted a playboy; a handsome playboy who would advertise his wealth, but one who could stay out of trouble. Both men had been disappointed. Page was lost and defeated, Paul looked contented.

"You know, Cinda," he said, taking off his cap and laying it on the bench beside him, "I have a hunch that Page may make it."

"I hope so." She leaned across the table to smile at him. "I do wish, though," she said, "that he were more like you. Daddy told us the other night that we have to learn to fly. Oh, Paul," she breathed, "I wish Page could be like you—and go soaring off in the right direction."

Her eyes were soft and wide as she tried to show him how sincere she was; but when he unexpectedly came forward at the same time, their faces almost touched.

Mercy! she thought, pleased. He's actually getting *personal.*

She felt "personal," herself, shut in by three sides of a cozy booth, her gaze locked with Paul's. Then Mr. Peterson sauntered in from the pharmacy room.

The sweet, secret current between them was broken, and they sat up very straight again. Paul picked up his cap, perched it on his light hair, and swept up the empty glasses. He looked as if he might break into a jolly whistle.

"I'll be back," he said, in the cocky, carefree way of Lindsey. "Don't fly away while I'm gone."

About the Author

Janet Lambert, beloved author of girls' fiction, was born and lived many years of her younger life in Crawfordsville, Indiana. Her hometown has been the home to many well known writers such as General Lew Wallace, author of Ben Hur. Prior to writing novels, the beautiful and talented Ms. Lambert performed as an actress and play writer touring with a repertory company around the United States and on Broadway. Her acting career was shortened during WWI by her marriage to then Captain Kent Lambert and later by the birth of her daughter, Jeanne Ann. As a perceptive and intellectually curious Army wife, Ms. Lambert gained insight into people, situations and life in many settings. These experiences were integrated into her writing for many years to come.

Janet Lambert's work has had and will continue to have a positive influence on the lives of "her girls" whom she loved so much.